Richard Garnett, Thomas Love Peacock

Calidore & miscellanea

Richard Garnett, Thomas Love Peacock

Calidore & miscellanea

ISBN/EAN: 9783337132231

Printed in Europe, USA, Canada, Australia, Japan

Cover: Foto ©Andreas Hilbeck / pixelio.de

More available books at **www.hansebooks.com**

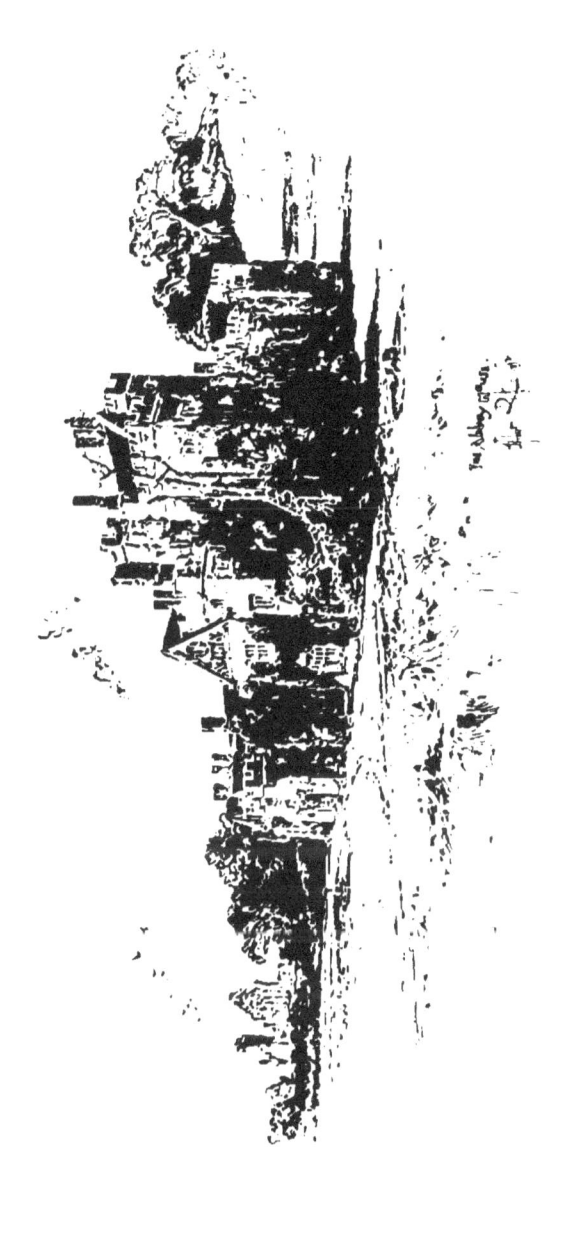

CALIDORE & MISCELLANEA

T. LOVE PEACOCK

EDITED BY
RICHARD GARNETT. LL.D.
AND PUBLISHED BY
J. M. DENT & Cº. AT ALDINE
HOUSE. 69. GREAT EASTERN ST.
LONDON. MDCCCXCI

CONTENTS.

INTRODUCTION.

"GATHER up the fragments that remain" is a precept whose application may be easily overstrained in the case of the literary remnants of a favourite author. A much smaller fraction than half is, in such instances, usually better than the whole. Peacock's editor and publisher, however, have agreed, and it is hoped that the body of his readers will not dissent, that the complete edition of his novels, which has now run its course, might be fitly supplemented by an appendix of minor writings, hitherto uncollected or not easily accessible. Such a decision is especially justifiable in the case of a writer whose slightest production bears the stamp of originality, and this is pre-eminently the case with Peacock, whose manner of presenting even a familiar idea is always distinctively his own. When his robust independence is associated with a congenial subject, the effect is very agreeable,—it is like being made thoroughly at home by one who is thoroughly at home himself. Peacock seldom responded to the mere call of a publisher or editor, for such a call was seldom addressed to him. He was neither

popular enough nor needy enough to be frequently
diverted from his own bent, and thus exempt from
taskwork, he could always be fresh and vigorous.
His reputation, it may be hoped, will not suffer
from any of the pieces comprised in the present
volume, some of which contribute new colour and
substance to the biographical outline of the author,
while others are essential to the full exhibition of
his character as a man of letters.

The first of these, however, is not from Peacock's
own pen. It is a paper of reminiscence, for which
the Editor is indebted to the unsolicited kindness
of Sir Edward Strachey, Bart., who, sixty years ago,
saw something and heard more of the Peacock of
the India House. The elder Strachey, known to
the readers of Carlyle as the subject of one of his
ineffaceable etchings of men of marked person-
ality, has a place in history as one of the ablest
home servants of the East India Company, who,
but for some impatience of the official harness,
might probably have risen to the highest place.
He was on cordial terms with his colleague, Peacock, and his son's reminiscences, as gracefully
written as they were gracefully tendered, contribute
something not only to their avowed purpose, but
to the record of the great City house from which
India was so long governed, which has not yet
found an historian.

"Some Recollections of Childhood," on the
other hand, are Peacock's own. They appeared
in *Bentley's Miscellany*, and were reprinted as

part of a short-lived series, entitled "Tales from Bentley." They exhibit the writer in a very amiable point of view, and afford an excellent illustration of the interest with which apparent trifles may be invested by one himself interested in them. In literature, as in painting, Millet's canon holds, that the chief thing to be considered is not so much the importance of the object as the genuineness of the artist's impulse. It is worthy of remark that a picture, entitled "Recollections of Childhood," was contributed by Peacock's old associate, Jefferson Hogg, to Bulwer's *Monthly Chronicle*, but only appeared there in part, for the same reason as that which abbreviated the ballad on the wise men of Gotham. "It was either too good or not good enough for the public taste," says Hogg, with an evident inclination to the former hypothesis.

"Calidore," a fragment of an unfinished romance, is the only absolute novelty from Peacock's pen in this volume. Several commencements of intended fictions exist in Peacock's papers; but, though written with as much care and finish as though they had received the author's last corrections for the press, they have in no other instance proceeded far enough to justify publication. They all belong to the latter portion of the author's life, with the exception of "Calidore," which was in all probability commenced shortly after the publication of "Melincourt." Like that work, it is an attempt to construct an elaborate fiction upon a basis only adequate to support a short story. If it had been compressed within the dimensions of Paul Heyse's "Centaur," a tale founded upon a similar idea, it might have been a considerable success, for it wants neither wit, humour, nor spirit; and the dialogue is more terse and pointed than usual. But the difficulty of working the conception out is tacitly admitted by the great hiatus in the MS. The Welsh adventures of the hero are suddenly dropped, and without so much as a rough draft to show how he got there, he is transferred to London, where a chapter, penned with as much elaboration as this singularly careful writer ever gave to anything, conducts to nothing at all. All the rest is boundless conjecture, *chimæra bombinans in vacuo.* What was written, however, excepting a small portion which has become obscure from the accidental imperfection of the MS., seems well worthy of preservation. It is highly characteristic of the author's enthusiasm for the past, and of the alliance which he would fain have effected between the classical spirit and the genius of romantic mediævalism, while interesting analogies may be traced between it and a more celebrated work inspired by a similar order of ideas, Heine's "Gods in Exile." The picture of the habits of Welsh parsons, utterly inapplicable at the present day, is probably derived from Peacock's acquaintance with the clergyman whom he describes in a letter as "a little, dumpy, drunken, mountain goat."

Peacock's " Four Ages of Poetry " has long ago

soared into immortality in the eagle grasp of the rejoinder which it provoked from Shelley, even though Shelley's specific references to it have been omitted. It is sufficiently manifest that if the author could have obtained an audience as a poet he would not have sought one as a critic, and the epithets whimsical and splenetic, may not seem quite inappropriate. On the other hand, the analysis of the birth, growth, and decay of poetry is both just and sagacious, so long as it is limited to a particular school or country, and it is understood that upon a comprehensive view these phenomena will ever be found simultaneous, like birth and death in the human race, or incandescence and extinction in the sidereal universe. It should further be remarked that the apparently illiberal treatment of the Lake Poets is far from expressing the writer's real sentiments. He delighted to gird at Wordsworth, Coleridge, and Southey, but he also delighted to quote them. In "Gryll Grange" he eulogises their absolute truth to Nature, and of Wordsworth he says, in an essay reprinted in this volume, "He has deep thought, graceful imaginings, great pathos, and little passion." —a judgment which, save that it ignores the inestimable service performed by the regeneration of poetic diction, may satisfy any but an ultra-Wordsworthian.

In "Horae Dramaticae," Peacock appears at his best as a critic. The themes are worth the labour, admitting of the eliciting of positive results, and

the reader lays the essays down with a conscious-
ness of distinct intellectual gain. Three ancient
dramas, one corrupt, one grievously mutilated, one
merely fragmentary, have been restored as perfectly
as circumstances permitted, a substantial conquest
from " the realm of Chaos and old Night."

" The Last Day of Windsor Forest " forms a
fitting conclusion to Peacock's writings, an old
man's reminiscence of an episode memorable in
the history of a place where much of his life had
been passed, and which, after his favourite river,
he loved better than any spot in the world. It
is also in all probability his last composition.
Written, as would seem, for *Fraser's Magazine*, it
was never sent there, and was first published by the
present writer in the *National Review* for August
1887.

Several others of Peacock's miscellaneous
articles would have borne reprinting, had the
dimensions of this volume allowed, and two, which
ought to be included in any future edition of his
writings pretending to completeness, are sufficiently
remarkable to demand a brief notice here. The
review of Moore's " Epicurean " in the *Westminster
Review* for October 1827, is really memorable. Peacock was not in general a very formidable assailant
of the men or opinions he disliked, but was for once
so thoroughly exasperated by Moore's caricature of
his favourite philosophy, " drawing a portrait of
everything that an eminent Epicurean was not, and
presenting it to us as a fair specimen of what he

was," and so well qualified by his own peculiar range of knowledge to effect and enjoy the exposure of Moore's misapprehensions as well as his misrepresentations, that he has for once achieved a criticism which may fairly be termed annihilating. He cannot, indeed, distil the corrosive acid of Carlyle, or unchain the overwhelming torrent of Macaulay; his indictment is cumulative; he returns to the charge again and again; and, if somewhat tardy in producing the desired effect, leaves his opponent at last riddled through and through with sarcasms. The following may serve as an example. Moore says :

> Among solitary columns and sphinxes, already half sunk from sight, Time seemed to stand waiting, till all that now flourished around should fall beneath his desolating hand like the rest.

Peacock comments :—

> The sands of the Libyan desert gaining on Memphis like a sea is an impressive though not original image, but the picture is altogether spoiled by the figure of Time standing waiting. Has Mr Moore forgotten that time and tide wait neither for men nor sands? The very essence of the idea of Time is steady, incessant, interminable progression. If he has any business in the place, it is as an agent, himself silently impelling the progress of desolation, not waiting till the sands have done their work, in order to begin his. And as Memphis was still a flourishing city at least four centuries later than our very curious specimen of an Epicurean, Time must have stood waiting for no inconsiderable portion of himself.

This may be a convenient place for recording that Peacock was the writer of two letters, signed

"Philatmos," in the *Times* of November 3 and November 7, 1838, on the unsuccessful attempt of the *Semiramis* in the previous July to steam against the monsoon from Bombay to Suez, which prove that any opposition on his part to the Red Sea route for the Indian mails was by no means due to any doubt of its practicability for steamships. There are probably other unacknowledged communications of his on the same subject.

RECOLLECTIONS

OF

THOMAS LOVE PEACOCK.

By Sir Edward Strachey, Bart.

————✱————

N the Examiner's Office at the India House
in Leadenhall Street, were drafted the
despatches of the Court of Directors of
the East India Company relating to the adminis-
tration of Justice, Revenue, and Public Works in
India.   In 1819 this Office was reorganised, with
a view to its greater efficiency, and three new men
—Edward Strachey (my father), James Mill, and
Thomas Love Peacock were introduced with the
title of " Assistants," to be employed in writing the
despatches in the above-mentioned departments
respectively.   They were thus brought into a
familiar intercourse, which, between my father and
Peacock, became a lasting friendship. My personal
recollections of Peacock do not go further back
than about 1827, but they were afterwards supplemented by those of my mother, and of my cousin,
the late Mrs Phillipps, known as Miss Kirkpatrick
to all readers of Thomas Carlyle's life.   I remember

Peacock in my father's room in the India House, and when he occasionally came to dine and sleep at our house at Shooter's Hill, as a kindly, genial, laughter-loving man, rather fond of good eating and drinking, or at least of talking as if he were so, for I remember no other actual proof of this than his saying, when asked if he would have some cherry pie, "That is one of my heresies," meaning that he ate it, though he knew it to be unwholesome; and it is possible that my recollections may be largely coloured by my familiarity with his descriptions of eating and drinking in the hospitable houses in his several novels. On the other hand, he practised as a young man, what his hero, Mr Forester in "Melincourt," preached, and gave up sugar as a protest against negro slavery. This my mother told me, my father having, I suppose, heard it from Peacock himself. She also told me that my father and one or two other friends were spending Saturday and Sunday with Peacock at his cottage when his little daughter died in 1826. The child was thought to be getting better, and Peacock went out in high spirits for a walk with his friends. When they came back he was told that the child was dead. His grief was great, and he said to my father that there were times when the world could not be made fun of. I remember my father bringing back one day the lines beginning " Long night succeeds thy little day," of which Peacock had just given him a copy, and which were put on the child's gravestone, as told by his grand-daughter.

James Mill, like Peacock, had his country walks
with his friends. Mrs Phillipps says, "James Mill
ordered one fine Sunday a beef-steak for dinner,
taking his ease at his inn, though not quite a Fal-
staff. The followers objected to the beef-steak
because it was very tough, and not otherwise
pleasant food. Mill said it was tender and good,
etc., because it was so and so, and therefore must
be tender." Peacock said, "Yes ; but, as usual,
all the reason is on your side, and all the proof on
mine." And again—Coulson, Editor of the *Globe*
and *Traveller*, said to Peacock, "When I know
Mill well, shall I like him—will he like what I like
and hate what I hate ? " " No," says Peacock,
"he will hate what you hate, and hate everything
you like." But this was too severe. For Coulson,
a friend of Charles Buller and of Frederick Maurice,
as well as of Peacock, could hardly have formed
the friendship which Professor Bain tells us existed
between him and Mill, on a common hatred only.
Mill was always kind to me when I saw him in my
father's room, yet the impression left on my mind
at the end of sixty years—an impression no doubt
made by what I was told as well as by what I saw
and heard—is a contrast to Peacock's place in
my memory as a warm-hearted, genial man, indulgent to himself, but not less indulgent to others.
It was from an unwillingness to show hospitality to
Mill that Peacock refrained from publishing the
volume of "Paper Money Lyrics," single pieces of
which, by degrees, appeared in the *Globe*, and else-

where, but of which I remember the MS. copy long
before. Though his humourous dislike of paper
money and political economists appears in his
earlier novels, it was no doubt much intensified
by his intercourse with Mill. He one day came
to my father's room, and said, with mock indigna-
tion, "I will never dine with Mill again, for he
asks me to meet only political economists. I dined
with him last night, when he had Mushet and
MacCulloch, and after dinner, Mushet took a
paper out of his pocket, and began to read : ' In
the infancy of society, when Government was invented to save a percentage—say, of 3½ per cent.'
—on which he was stopped by MacCulloch with,
' I will say no such thing,' meaning that this was
not the proper percentage." Two or three years
later, the story was told in "Crotchet Castle" in
the way the reader knows. Peacock was pleased
when he was told that a boy's simplicity had
vainly tried to make out which of his characters
represented his own opinions, saying : "That is
just as it should be." But my father told me he
thought that Peacock really considered the state of
society when men wore armour and had no paper
money, was better than our own. But he used to
quote, with approval, the classical saying that the
world was *flebile ludibrium*, and he probably cared
less for the relative merits of different periods
of history, than for the suitableness of each for
supplying the materials for fun and laughter. He
satirised the vices and follies of men as a fun-loving

caricaturist more than as a Juvenal or a Butler, though the sterner mood is not always absent; and his caricatures of Shelley, Byron, Southey, Wordsworth, Coleridge, and the editors of the *Quarterly* and *Edinburgh Reviews* provoke our laughter by the ridiculous want of resemblance to their originals. He scoffed impartially at the two great party *Reviews*, and once he said to my father, as they passed a man with a package of *Edinburgh Reviews*, " There goes a lot of lies and bad grammar," with as much pleasure as if he had been the editor of the *Legitimate Review*, to whom he has introduced us in " Melincourt."

Peacock loved Latin and Greek, Italian and French literature, as well as that of England. There is a story of his familiarity with French, and his ready wit (reminding us of a somewhat similar story of Sheridan), how he recited, in discussing with a Frenchman the tragic dignity of Racine, several lines, beginning with " Madame préparez votre mouchoir; " and the unsuspecting hearer could only reply—" Ah, sir, you have taken the very worst verses in all Racine." In his " Misfortunes of Elphin," he gave the Welsh legends with careful accuracy. I heard him say that he had great difficulty in getting at the true story of Taliesin's birth, as more than one learned authority had concealed his own ignorance on the matter by saying that the story was too long to be told then ; and he was proud of the fact that Welsh archæologists treated his book as a serious and valuable

addition to Welsh history. His familiar love of
Latin and Greek is known to all his readers. Many
a scholar must have found a new pleasure in his
out-of-the-way quotations and allusions, and in the
skilful humour of his Greek etymologies of English
names, and especially for those of the three philosophers in " Headlong Hall," than which nothing
could be happier. Like other men who have never
been at Oxford or Cambridge, he would speak dis-
paragingly of the learning of those Universities, and
avowed his opinion of the superiority of the Germans
in classical studies. But though he recommended
me a German commentary on Greek metres as
better than those of any English critic, he put
Maltby's Lexicon as one of the three Greek
Lexicons which, he told my father, were indispensable for me, the other two being Hedericus
and Scapula, and he finally himself selected for
me a copy of the London edition of Scapula,
edited in 1820 by the English scholars Bailey
and Major. It was pardonable if there was a
little mixture of vanity in Peacock's assertion
that the Dionysiaca of Nonnus was the finest poem
in the world after the Iliad, since very few but
himself had the knowledge of the former which
could qualify them for deciding or discussing the
question on its merits. The highly-polished verse
of the Panopolitan poet would have greater charms
for a man of Peacock's generation than for our own,
and the two specimens which he gives as mottoes
to chapters viii. and x. of the " Misfortunes of

Elphin" can hardly be praised too much for their grace and beauty. I may be forgiven if, in my eightieth year, I look back to the day when Peacock sent, through my father, the verses which make me fond of these mottoes,* to the schoolboy in whose studies he took so kind an interest.

Peacock's literary style was elaborately polished, and he disliked writing letters, lest he should fall into any fault in hasty composition. His official despatches were described by my father as "neat and exact, characteristic of the man." Whether "the Chairs" in Leadenhall Street or the Board of Control found any wit or humour in them I know not: but I recall Peacock's account of his having gone one day to see a director of the Company sell tea. He found the great merchant prince sitting at a table in a room, round which were a number of tea brokers in a state of fury, each brandishing a huge ledger, and occasionally shouting out, "A halfpenny." The monopoly of tea, of

---

* Ἀλλὰ τεαῖς παλάμῃσι μαχήμονα θύρσον ἀείρων,
Αἰθέρος ἄξια ῥέξον· ἐπεὶ Διὸς ἄμβροτος αὐλὴ
Οὔ σε πόνων ἀπάνευθε δεδέξεται· οὐδέ σοι Ὧραι
Μήπω ἀεθλεύσαντι πύλας πετάσωσιν Ὀλύμπου.

Grasp the bold thyrsus; seek the field's array;
And do things worthy of ethereal day:
Not without toil to earthborn man befalls
To tread the floors of Jove's immortal halls:
Never to him, who not by deeds has striven,
Will the bright Hours roll back the gates of heaven.

IRIS TO BACCHUS, *in the 13th Book of the*
DIONYSIACA OF NONNUS.

which the lowest price was eight shillings a pound,
gave the East India Company a revenue sufficient
to pay the whole of the home expenses of the Company, including the interest on their stock, and also
to pay a like sum into the British treasury.

If, in conclusion, I may supplement these imperfect memories and family traditions from the
sources of Peacock's books and the memoirs of
his grand-daughter, I should say that he was a
kind-hearted, genial, friendly man, who loved to
share his enjoyment of life with all around him ;
and he was self-indulgent without being selfish.
His ideals of life were noble and generous, and in
" Melincourt " they temper with seriousness, even
sadness, the boyish love of fun and caricature which
never fail him. And if we see in " The Misfortunes
of Elphin " and " Crotchet Castle " increased intellectual power accompanied by a more worldly
tone of thought, the natural consequence of prosperous enjoyment of life as he found it, it is pleasant
to recognise signs in " Gryll Grange," the child of
his old age, a softer and better morality than that
which characterises the two last-named books.

I have written down these reminiscences of
Thomas Love Peacock honestly : but I do not ask
the reader to accept them as absolutely true. A
good memory implies a sufficient activity of imagination to form our original impressions of a person
or an event into a distinct picture. And then we
keep that picture clear and living in our mind's
eye by retouching it from time to time by what we

suppose to be memory, but which is often, in great part at least, imagination. And so, year after year, we recollect our last recollections, and not the original thing itself, or even its first image. The process is unconscious, but we occasionally discover its reality when we come across some contemporary or otherwise independent record, and find how much is different from our own. The proper title of a biography, whether of oneself or of another, will probably always be " Dichtung und Wahrheit," if we translate it " Truth and Fiction," and not necessarily " Poetry and Truth."

EDWARD STRACHEY.

RECOLLECTIONS OF CHILDHOOD.

By the Author of "Headlong Hall."

———✱———

The Abbey House.

PASSED many of my early days in a country town, on whose immediate outskirts stood an ancient mansion, bearing the name of the Abbey House. This mansion has long since vanished from the face of the earth ; but many of my pleasantest youthful recollections are associated with it, and in my mind's eye I still see it as it stood, with its amiable, simple-mannered, old English inhabitants.

The house derived its name from standing near, though not actually on, the site of one of those rich old abbeys, whose demesnes the pure devotion of Henry the Eighth transferred from their former occupants (who foolishly imagined they had a right to them, though they lacked the might which is its essence) to the members of his convenient Parliamentary chorus, who helped him to run down his Scotch octave of wives. Of the abbey itself a very small portion remained : a gateway, a piece of a wall which formed part of the enclosure of an orchard, wherein a curious series of fish ponds, connected by sluices, was fed from a contiguous stream with a perpetual circulation of fresh water, a sort of piscatorial panopticon, where all approved varieties of fresh-water fish had been classified, each in its own pond, and kept in good order, clean and fat, for the mortification of the flesh of the monastic brotherhood on fast days.

The road which led to the Abbey House terminated. as a carriage road with the house itself. Beyond it, a footpath over meadows conducted across a ferry to a village about a mile distant. A large clump of old walnut trees stood on the opposite side of the road to a pair of massy iron gates, which gave entrance to a circular gravel road, encompassing a large smooth lawn, with a sun-dial in the centre, and bordered on both sides with tall, thick evergreens and flowering shrubs, interspersed in the seasons with hollyhocks, sunflowers, and other gigantic blossoms, such as are splendid in distances. Within, immediately opposite the gates, a broad flight of stone steps led to a ponderous portal, and to a large antique hall, laid with a chequered pavement of black and white marble. On the left side of the entrance was the porter's chair, consisting of a cushioned seat, occupying the depth of a capacious recess, resembling a niche for a full-sized statue, a well-stuffed body of black leather glittering with gold-

headed nails.   On the right of this hall was the
great staircase ; on the left, a passage to a wing
appropriated to the domestics.

Facing the portal, a door opened into an inner
hall, in the centre of which was a billiard table.
On the right of this hall was a library ; on the left
a parlour, which was the common sitting-room ;
and facing the middle was a glazed door, opening
on the broad flight of stone steps which led into
the gardens.

The gardens were in the old style : a large,
square lawn occupied an ample space in the
centre, separated by broad walks from belts of
trees and shrubs on each side ; and in front
were two advancing groves, with a long, wide
vista between them, looking to the open country,
from which the grounds were separated by a ter-
raced wall over a deep, sunken dyke.   One of the
groves we called the Green Grove and the other
the Dark Grove.   The first had a pleasant glade,
with sloping banks covered with flowery turf ; the
other was a mass of trees, too closely canopied with
foliage for grass to grow beneath them.

The family consisted of a gentleman and his
wife, with two daughters and a son.   The eldest
daughter was on the confines of womanhood ; the
youngest was little more than a child ; the son was
between them.   I do not know his exact age, but
I was seven or eight, and he was two or three years
more.

The family lived, from taste, in a very retired

manner; but to the few whom they received they were eminently hospitable. I was, perhaps, the foremost among these few, for Charles, who was my schoolfellow, was never happy in our holidays unless I was with him. A frequent guest was an elderly male relation, much respected by the family, but no favourite of Charles, over whom he was disposed to assume greater authority than Charles was willing to acknowledge.

The mother and daughter had all the solid qualities which were considered female virtues in the dark ages. Our enlightened age has, wisely, no doubt, discarded many of them, and substituted show for solidity. The dark ages preferred the natural blossom, and the fruit that follows it; the enlightened age prefers the artificial double-blossom, which falls and leaves nothing. But the double-blossom is brilliant while it lasts; and where there is much light there ought to be something to glitter in it.

These ladies had the faculty of staying at home; and this was a principle among the antique faculties that upheld the rural mansions of the middling gentry. Ask Brighton, Cheltenham, *et id genus omne*, what has become of that faculty. And ask the plough-share what has become of the rural mansions.

They never, I think, went out of their own grounds but to church, or to take their regular daily airing in the old family carriage. The young lady was an adept in preserving: she had one room, in

the corner of the hall, between the front and the
great staircase, entirely surrounded with shelves in
compartments stowed with classified sweetmeats,
jellies, and preserved fruits, the work of her own
sweet hands. These were distinguished ornaments
of the supper-table ; for the family dined early, and
maintained the old fashion of supper. A child
would not easily forget the bountiful and beautiful
array of fruits, natural and preserved, and the
ample variety of preparations of milk, cream, and
custard, by which they were accompanied. The
supper-table had matter for all tastes. I remember
what was most to mine.

The young lady performed on the harpsichord.
Over what a gulf of time this name alone looks
back ! What a stride from the harpsichord to one
of Broadwood's last grand pianos ! And yet with
what pleasure, as I stood by the corner of the instrument, I listened to it, or rather, to her ! I
would give much to know that the worldly lot of
this gentle and amiable creature had been a happy
one. She often gently remonstrated with me for
putting her harpsichord out of tune by playing the
bells upon it ; but I was never in a serious scrape
with her, except once. I had insisted on taking
from the nursery maid the handle of the little girl's
garden carriage, with which I set off at full speed,
and had not run many yards before I overturned
the carriage, and rolled out the little girl. The
child cried like Alice Fell, and would not be
pacified. Luckily she ran to her sister, who let

me off with an admonition, and the exaction of a promise never to meddle again with the child's carriage.

Charles was fond of romances. The "Mysteries of Udolpho," and all the ghost and goblin stories of the day, were his familiar reading. I cared little about them at that time; but he amused me by relating their grimmest passages. He was very anxious that the Abbey House should be haunted, but it had no strange sights or sounds, and no plausible tradition to hang a ghost on. I had very nearly accommodated him with what he wanted.

The garden-front of the house was covered with jasmine, and it was a pure delight to stand in the summer twilight on the top of the stone steps inhaling the fragrance of the multitudinous blossoms. One evening, as I was standing on these steps alone, I saw something like the white head-dress of a tall figure advancing from the right-hand grove,—the Dark Grove as we called it—and, after a brief interval, recede. This, at anyrate, looked awful. Presently it appeared again, and again vanished. On which I jumped to my conclusion, and flew into the parlour with the announcement that there was a ghost in the Dark Grove. The whole family sallied forth to see the phenomenon. The appearances and disappearances continued. All conjectured what it could be, but none could divine. In a minute or two all the servants were in the hall. They all tried their skill, and were all equally unable to solve the riddle. At last, the master of the house leading the way, we marched in a body to the spot, and unravelled the mystery. It was a large bunch of flowers on the top of a tall lily, waving in the wind at the edge of the grove, and disappearing at intervals behind the stem of a tree. My ghost, and the compact phalanx in which we sallied against it, were long the subject of merriment. It was a cruel disappointment to Charles, who was obliged to abandon all hopes of having the house haunted.

One day Charles was in disgrace with his elder relation, who had exerted sufficient authority to make him a captive in his chamber. He was prohibited from seeing any one but me; and, of course, a most urgent messenger was sent to me express. I found him in his chamber, sitting by the fire, with a pile of ghostly tales, and an accumulation of lead, which he was casting into dumps in a mould. Dumps, the inexperienced reader must know, are flat circles of lead—a sort of petty quoits—with which schoolboys amused themselves half a century ago, and perhaps do still, unless the march of mind has marched off with such vanities. No doubt, in the "astounding progress of intellect," the time will arrive when boys will play at philosophers instead of playing at soldiers—will fight with wooden arguments instead of wooden swords —and pitch leaden syllogisms instead of leaden dumps. Charles was before the dawn of this new light. He had cast several hundred dumps, and was still at work. The quibble did not occur to me at the time; but, in after years, I never heard of a man in the dumps without thinking of my schoolfellow. His position was sufficiently melancholy. His chamber was at the end of a long corridor. He was determined not to make any submission, and his captivity was likely to last till the end of his holidays. Ghost stories, and lead for dumps, were his stores and provisions, for standing the siege of *ennui*. I think, with the aid of his sister, I had some share in making his peace; but such is the association of ideas, that, when I first read in Lord Byron's Don Juan,

> "I pass my evenings in long galleries solely,
> And that's the reason I'm so melancholy;"

the lines immediately conjured up the image of poor Charles in the midst of his dumps and spectres at the end of his own long gallery.

CALIDORE: A FRAGMENT OF
A ROMANCE. [1816?]

——✱——

CHAPTER I.

NOTWITHSTANDING the great improvements of machinery in this rapidly improving age, which is so much wiser, better, and happier than all that went before it, every gentleman is not yet accommodated with the convenience of a pocket boat. We may therefore readily imagine that Miss Ap-Nanny and her sister Ellen, the daughters of the Vicar of Llanglasrhyd, were not a little astonished in a Sunday evening walk on the sea shore, when a little skiff, which, by the rapidity of its motion had attracted their attention while but a speck upon the waves, ran upon the beach, from which emerged a very handsome young gentleman, dressed not exactly in the newest fashion, who, after taking down the sail and hauling up the boat upon the beach, carefully folded it up in the size of a prayer-book and transferred it to his pocket. He did not notice the young ladies till he had completed this operation, and when he looked round and discovered them he seemed a little confused, but made them a very courteous bow in a fine but rather singular style of ancient politeness. From the moment of his first landing, and the commencement of the curious process of folding up his boat, Miss Ap-Nanny had been dying with curiosity, and had consulted her sister Ellen as to the propriety of addressing the stranger, having, however, fully made up her mind before-hand as usual with young ladies when they ask advice.

The inn was filled with picturesque tourists who had arrived in various vehicles by the help of those noble quadrupeds who confer so much dignity on the insignificant biped, that if he venture to travel without them and rest his reception on his own merits the difference of his welcome may serve to show him how much more of his imaginary im-portance belongs to his horse than to himself. Our traveller arriving alone and on foot was received with half a courtesy by the landlady, and shown into the common parlour where the incipient cold of the autumnal evening was dispelled by an im-mense turf fire, by which were sitting two elderly gentlemen of the clerical profession, recumbent in arm chairs, with their eyes half shut, and their legs stretched out so that the points of their shoes came in contact at the centre of the fender. Each was smoking his pipe with contemplative gravity. Neither spoke nor moved, except now and then as

if by mechanism, to fill his glass from the jug of
ale that stood between them on the table, and the
moment this good example was set by one the
other followed it instantaneously and automatically
as the two figures at St Dunstan's strike upon the
bell to the great delight of Cockneys, amazement
of rustics, and consolation of pickpockets. The
stranger made several attempts to draw them into
conversation, but could not succeed in extracting
more than a " hum " from either of them. At length
one of the reverend gentlemen, having buzzed the
jug, articulated, with slow and minute emphasis :
" Will you join in another jug ? "   " Hum ! " said
the other. A violent rattling of copper ensued in
their respective coat pockets ; two equal quantities
of half-pence were deliberately counted down upon
the table ; the bell was rung, and the little, round,
Welsh waiting-maid carried out the money, and
replenished the jug in silence. They went on as
before till the liquor was exhausted, when it became the other's turn to ask the question, and the
same eventful words, " Will you join in another
jug ? " were repeated, with the same ceremonies and
the same results. Our traveller, in the meanwhile,
looked over his tablets of instruction. These two
reverend gentlemen were the Vicar of Llanglasrhyd
and the Rector of Bwlchpenbach. The rector performed afternoon service at a chapel twenty miles
from his rectory, and Llanglasrhyd lying half-way
between them, he slept every Sunday night under
the roof of Gwyneth Owen, where his dearest friend,

the Vicar of Llanglasrhyd, met him to smoke away the evening. They had thus passed together every Sunday evening for forty years, and during the whole period had scarcely said ten words to each other beyond the usual forms of meeting and parting, and "Will you join in another jug?" Yet were their meetings so interwoven with their habitual comforts that either would have regarded the loss of the other as the greatest earthly misfortune that could have befallen him, and would never, perhaps, have mustered sufficient firmness of voice to address the same question, "Will you join in another jug?" to any other human being. It may seem singular to those who have heard the extensive form of Welsh hospitality that the vicar did not invite the rector to pass these evenings at his vicarage; but it must be remembered that the Rector of Bwlchpenbach was every week at Llanglasrhyd in the way of his business, and that the Vicar of Llanglasrhyd had no business whatever to take him on any single occasion to Bwlchpenbach ; therefore the balance of the consumption of ale would have been entirely against the vicar, and as they regularly drank three quarts each at a sitting, or one hundred and fifty-six quarts in a year, the Rector of Bwlchpenbach would have consumed in forty years six thousand two hundred and forty quarts of ale, without equivalent or compensation, at the expense of the Vicar of Llanglasrhyd, a circumstance not to be thought of without vexation of spirit.

Our traveller folded up his tablets, rung the bell,

and inquired what he could have for supper, and
what wine was to be had ? The landlady entered
with a tempting list of articles, and enumerated
several names of wine. The stranger seemed per-
plexed, and at length said he would have them all,
for he liked to see a well-covered table, having
always been used to one. The landlady dropped
a double courtesy, and the reverend gentlemen
dropped their pipes ; the pipes broke, and the
odorous embers were scattered on the hearth.

When the supper smoked, and the wine sparkled
on the table, the stranger pressed the reverend
gentlemen to join him. They did not indeed
require much pressing, and assisted with great
industry in the demolition of his abundant banquet :
but still not a syllable could he extract from either
of them except that the Vicar of Llanglasrhyd,
when his heart was warmed with Madeira, invited
the rector and the young stranger to breakfast with
him the next morning at the vicarage, which the
latter joyfully accepted, as he very well by this time
understood that his lively and jovial companion
was the father of the beautiful creature who had
charmed him on the sea-shore. He sate from this
time in contented silence, contemplating the happy
meeting of the following morning while the reverend gentlemen sipped the liquid so far and only till
with their usual felicitous sympathy they vanished
at the same instant under the table. The landlady
and her household were summoned to their assistance. The Vicar of Llanglasrhyd was carried home

by the postillions, and the Rector of Bwlchpenbach
was put to bed by the ostler.

.   .   .   .   .   .

Allow me to hand you some toast : you must
have had a very pleasant sail yesterday.—Very
pleasant !—Did you come far ? Very far.—From
Ireland perhaps.—Not from Ireland.—Then you
must have come a long way in such a small boat,
such a very small boat.—Not so very small : it is one
of our best sea boats.—Do you carry your best sea
boats in your waistcoat pockets ?   Then I suppose
in your great-coat pockets you carry your ships of
the line.—But, dear me, sir, you must come from
a very strange place.—I come from a part of the
world which is known to the rest by the name of
Terra Incognita.   I am not at liberty to say more
concerning it.—But, sir, if it is a fair question, what
has brought you to Wales ?— I have landed on this
shore by accident.   My present destination is
London.   I am to remain in this island twelve
months, and return with a wife and a philosopher.
—God bless me ! what can Terra Incognita want
with a philosopher, and how are you to take them
away ?—In the same boat that brought me.—Why,
who do you think will trust herself?   You would
like some more tea ?—Ellen, my dear, do you think
any lady would trust herself?—If she had love
enough, said Ellen.—Cream and sugar, said Miss
Ap-Nanny.—The boat is perfectly safe, said the
stranger, looking at Ellen.   I could go through a
hurricane with it.—Love, to be sure, will do any-

thing, said Miss Ap-Nanny, but, Lord bless me ! I may take an egg, and to be sure it would be worth some risk just in the way of curiosity to see Terra Incognita. They must be very strange people, but what they can want of a philosopher I cannot imagine.—I hope if you bring him this way you will keep him muzzled, for my papa says they are very terrible monsters, fiends of darkness and imps of the devil. I would not trust myself in a boat with one for the world. Would you, Ellen, my dear?—I should not be much afraid, said Ellen, smiling, if he were in the hands of a safe keeper. —We have a philosopher or two among us already, said the stranger, and they are by no means such formidable animals as you seem to suppose.—But my papa says so, said Miss Ap-Nanny.—I bow acquiescence, said the stranger, but perhaps the Welsh variety is a peculiarly fierce breed.—I am happy to say there is not one in all Wales, said Miss Ap-Nanny.—I hear they run tame in London, said Ellen.—Then you are not so much afraid of them as your sister, said the stranger.—Not quite, said Ellen, smiling again, I think I would venture into the same room with one even if he were not in an iron cage.—Oh, fie, Ellen, said Miss Ap-Nanny, that is what you call having liberal opinions. I cannot imagine where you got them. I am sure you did not learn them from me. Do you know, sir, Ellen is very heterodox. My papa actually detected her in the fact of reading a wicked book called "Principles of Moral Science," which, with his usual sweet temper, he put, without saying a word, behind the fire. He says liberal opinions are only another name for impiety.—Dear, good man ! said Mrs Ap-Nanny, opening her mouth for the first time, he never was guilty of a liberal opinion in the course of his life.

.   .   .   .   .

Sir, what can a young man of your figure—you look like a courtier—mean by making love at first sight to my daughter ? What can you mean, sir ? Perhaps you have heard that she will have a thousand pounds, and that may be a temptation. —Money, said the stranger, is to me mere chaff ; and producing a bag from his pocket, and shaking it by one corner, he scattered on the floor a profusion of gold. The Vicar, who had seen nothing but paper money for twenty years, was astonished at these yellow apparitions, and picking up one inspected it with great curiosity. On one side was the phenomenon of a crowned head with a handsome and intelligent face, and the legend ARTHURUS REX. On the reverse, a lion sleeping at Neptune's feet, and the legend REDIBO.—Here is a foreign potentate, said the Reverend Dr Ap-Nanny, whom I never remember to have heard of. Pray, is he legitimate by the grace of God, or a blasphemous and seditious usurper whom the people have had the impudence to choose for themselves?—He is very legitimate and has an older title than any other being in the world. —Then I reverence him, said the Vicar. Old

Authority, sir, old Authority, there is nothing like old Authority. But what do you want with my daughter?—Candidly, sir, said the stranger, I am on a quest for a wife, and am so far inspired by the grace of Venus, Cupid, and Juno, that I am willing my quest should end where it begins—here. —On a quest, exclaimed the Vicar ; Venus, Cupid, and Juno ! Ah ! I see how it is. Rich, humoured, and touched in the head. Pray, what do you mean by Juno ?—Juno Pronuba, said the stranger, the goddess of marriage.—I see, sir, you are inclined to make a joke of both me and my daughter. Sir, I must tell you this very unbecoming levity.—My dear sir, I assure you.—Sir, it is palpable. Would any man make a serious proposal to a man of my cloth for his daughter, and talk to him of the grace of Venus and Cupid and Juno Pronuba, the goddess of marriage ?—I swear to you, sir, said the stranger, earnestly, by the sacred head of Pan.

.   .   .   .   .

When they approached the destined island they were delighted to perceive that its aspect presented a most promising diversity of mountain, valley, and forest reposing in the sunshine of a delicious climate. Two very singular persons were walking on the seashore ; one in the appearance a young and handsome man with a crown of vine-leaves on his head ; the other a wild and singular figure in a fine state of picturesque roughness with goat's horns and feet and a laughing face. As the vessel fixed its keel in the shore and King Arthur and his party landed, the two strangers approached and inquired who they were, and whence they came?—This, replied Merlin, is the great King Arthur; this is his fair queen, Guenevere: and I am the potent Merlin: these are the illustrious knights of the round table: and this is the King's butler, Bedevere. The butler, said the first stranger, shall be welcome. And so shall the ladies, said the second. But as to the rest of you, pursued the first, we must know you a little better before we accord you our permission to advance a step in this island. I am Bacchus, and I, said the other, am Pan. So, said Sir Launcelot, I find we have to contend with the evil powers. If you mean us by that appellation, said Bacchus, you will find us too strong for you. This island is the retreat of all the gods and goddesses, genii and nymphs, who formerly reigned in Olympus, and dwelt in the mountains and valleys of Greece and Italy. Though we had not much need of mankind, we had a great affection for them, and lived among them on good terms and in an interchange of kind offices. They regaled us with the odours of sacrifice, built us magnificent temples, and especially showed their piety by singing and dancing, and being always social and cheerful, and full of pleasure and life, which is the most gratifying appearance that man can present to the gods. But after a certain time they began to change most lamentably for the worse. They discontinued their

sacrifices; they broke our images, many of which
we had sate for ourselves; they called us frightful
and cacophonous names—Beelzebub and Amaimon
and Astaroth : they plundered and demolished
our temples, and built ugly structures on their
ruins, where, instead of dancing and rejoicing as
they had been used to do, and delighting us with
spectacles of human happiness, they were eternally
sighing and groaning, and beating their breasts,
and dropping their lower jaws, and turning up the
whites of their eyes, and cursing each other and
all mankind, and chaunting such dismal staves
that we shut our eyes and ears, and, flying from
our favourite terrestrial scenes, assembled in a
body among the clouds of Olympus. Here we
held a council as to what was to be done for the
amendment of these perverted mortals; but Jupiter
informed us that necessity, his mistress, and that
of the world, compelled him to acquiesce for a
time in this condition of things, that mankind, who
had never been good for a great deal, were now
become so worthless, and withal so disagreeable,
that the wisest course we could adopt would be to
leave them to themselves and retire to an undisturbed island for which he had stipulated with the
fates.   Here, then, we are, and have been for
ages.   That mountain on which the white clouds
are resting is now Mount Olympus, and there
dwell Jupiter and the Olympian deities. In these
forests and valleys reside Pan and Silenus, the
Fauns and the Satyrs, and the small nymphs and

genii. I divide my time between the two, for though my home is Olympus, I have a most special friendship for Pan. Now I have only this to say, that if you come here to make frightful faces, chaunt long tunes, and curse each other through the nose, I give you fair warning to depart in peace : if not, we shall find no trouble in expelling you by force, as Jupiter will testify to you. Jupiter gave the required testification by a peal of thunder from Olympus.

Merlin and King Arthur fell on their knees, and the rest of their party followed the example. Great Bacchus and mighty Pan, said Merlin, pity our ignorance and take us under your protection, for if you banish us from this happy shore, our vessel must wander over the seas for ever, like the Flying Dutchman that is to be, and we are very ill victualled for such a navigation.

    .   .   .   .   .   .

The first object of Calidore on arriving in London was to change some of his gold Arthurs into the circulating medium of the country, and on making inquiry at his hotel, he was directed, for this purpose, to a spacious stone building with high walls and no windows. Alighting from his hackney-coach, with a money-box in his hand, he wandered through a labyrinth of paved courts and spacious rooms filled with smoky-faced clerks and solid globes of Jews, through some of which he had great difficulty in forcing his way. After some time, he discovered the office he wanted, presented his gold, which was duly tried, weighed, and carefully removed from his sight. The sum was enounced with very distinct articulation, and a piece of paper was given to him, with which he was sent to another place. How would you like it, sir? said a little sharp-nosed man with a quill behind his ear.—In the circulating medium of this city, said Calidore.—But I mean, sir, in what portions?—In no portions : I wish to have it all at once.—Thousands, sir? said the little man.—The specified sum, sir, said Calidore.—The little man put into his hand several slips of paper.—Well, sir ! said Calidore, what am I to do with these?—Whatever you please, sir, said the little man, smiling. I wish I could say as much for myself.— I am much obliged to you, said Calidore ; and I have no doubt you are an exceedingly facetious and agreeable person ; but, at the same time, if you would have the goodness to direct me where I can receive my money——Sir, said the little man, that is your money.—This !—Certainly, sir ; that. What would you have ?—Gold coin, to be sure, said Calidore.—Gold coin ! I am afraid, sir, you are a disaffected man and a Jacobin, or you would not ask for such a thing, when I have given you the best money in the world. Pray, sir, look at it— you are a stranger, perhaps—look at it, sir; that's all. —Calidore looked at one of the pieces of paper, and read aloud : I promise to pay to Mr Henry Hare — One Thousand Pounds — John Figginbotham.—Well, sir ; and what have I to do with

John Figginbotham's promise to pay a thousand pounds to Henry Hare?—John Figginbotham, sir, having made that promise, and put it upon that paper, makes that paper worth a thousand pounds. —To Henry Hare, said Calidore.—To any one, said the little man. You overlook the words : or bearer. Now, sir, you are the bearer.—I understand. John Figginbotham promises to pay me a thousand pounds.—Precisely.—Then, sir, if you will have the goodness to direct me to John Figginbotham I will thank him to pay me directly. —But, good God, sir ! you mistake the matter.— Mistake, sir !—Yes, sir ! John Figginbotham does not pay ; he only signs. We pay : we, who are here ; I and my chums.—Very well, sir ; then why can you not pay me without all this circumlocution ? —Sir, I have paid you.—How, sir ?—With those notes, sir. Sir, these are promises to pay, made by one Figginbotham. I wish these promises to be performed. You send me round in a circle from Hare to Figginbotham, and from Figginbotham to yourself, and I am still as much in the dark as ever, as to where I am to look for the performance of their very liberal promises.—Oh ! the performance, sir,—very true sir,—as you say ; but, sir, promises are of two kinds, those which are meant to be performed, and those which are not, the latter being forms used for convenience and dispatch of business.—Then, sir, these promises are not meant to be performed.—Pardon me, sir, they are meant to be performed, not literally, but in a

manner. They used to be performed by giving
gold to the bearer, but that having been found
peculiarly inconvenient has been laid aside by Act
of Parliament ever since the year Ninety-Seven, and
we now pay paper with paper, which simplifies
business exceedingly.—And pray, sir, do these
promises to pay pass for realities among the people ?
—Certainly they do, sir; one of those slips of
paper which you hold in your hand will purchase
the labour of fifty men for a year.—John Figginbotham must be a person of very great consequence, there is not much trouble I presume in
making one of these things.—Not much, sir.—
Then I suppose, sir, John Figginbotham has all the
labour of the country under his absolute disposal.
Assuredly this Figginbotham must be a great
magician, and profoundly skilled in magic and
demonology: for this is almost more than Merlin
could do, to make the eternal repetition of the
same promise pass for its eternal performance,
and exercise unlimited control over the lives and
fortunes of a whole nation, merely by putting his
name upon pieces of paper. However, since,
such is the case, I must try to make the best of the
matter: but if I find that these talismans of the
great magician Figginbotham do not act upon the
people as you give me to understand they will,
I shall take the liberty of blowing my bugle in his
enchanted castle, and in the meantime, sir, I
respectfully take leave of your courtly presence.
—Poor, deranged gentleman ! exclaimed the little

man after Calidore was gone, did you ever hear a man talk so in all your life, Mr Solomons?—Very much cracked, said Mr Solomons, very much cracked in the head; but seems to be sound in the pocket, which is the better part of man.

MISCELLANIES.

[*Published in Ollier's Miscellany*, 1820.]

———✳———

THE FOUR AGES OF POETRY.

Qui inter hæc nutriuntur non magis sapere possunt, quam bene olere qui in culinâ habitant.—PETRONIUS.

POETRY, like the world, may be said to have four ages, but in a different order: the first age of poetry being the age of iron ; the second, of gold ; the third, of silver ; and the fourth of brass.

The first, or iron age of poetry, is that in which rude bards celebrate in rough numbers the exploits of ruder chiefs, in days when every man is a warrior, and when the great practical maxim of every form of society, " to keep what we have and to catch what we can," is not yet disguised under names of justice and forms of law, but is the naked motto of the naked sword, which is the only judge and jury in every question of *meum* and *tuum*. In these days, the only three trades flourishing (besides that of priest, which flourishes always) are those of king, thief, and beggar : the beggar being, for the most part, a king deject, and the thief a king expectant. The first question asked of a stranger is, whether he is a beggar or a thief :* the stranger, in reply, usually assumes the first, and awaits a convenient opportunity to prove his claim to the second appellation.

The natural desire of every man to engross to himself as much power and property as he can acquire by any of the means which might makes right, is accompanied by the no less natural desire of making known to as many people as possible the extent to which he has been a winner in this universal game. The successful warrior becomes a chief; the successful chief becomes a king : his next want is an organ to disseminate the fame of his achievements and the extent of his possessions ; and this organ he finds in a bard, who is always ready to celebrate the strength of his arm, being first duly inspired by that of his liquor. This is the origin of poetry, which, like all other trades, takes its rise in the demand for the commodity, and flourishes in proportion to the extent of the market.

Poetry is thus in its origin panegyrical. The first rude songs of all nations appear to be a sort of brief historical notices, in a strain of tumid hyperbole, of the exploits and possessions of a few pre-eminent individuals. They tell us how many battles such an one has fought, how many helmets he has cleft, how many breastplates he has pierced, how many widows he has made, how much land he

* See the Odyssey, passim : and Thucydides, I. 5.

has appropriated, how many houses he has demolished for other people, what a large one he has
built for himself, how much gold he has stowed
away in it, and how liberally and plentifully he
pays, feeds, and intoxicates the divine and immortal bards, the sons of Jupiter, but for whose
everlasting songs the names of heroes would
perish.

This is the first stage of poetry before the inven-
tion of written letters. The numerical modulation
is at once useful as a help to memory, and pleasant
to the ears of uncultured men, who are easily
caught by sound : and, from the exceeding flexibility of the yet unformed language, the poet does
no violence to his ideas in subjecting them to the
fetters of number. The savage, indeed, lisps in
numbers, and all rude and uncivilised people
express themselves in the manner which we call
poetical.

The scenery by which he is surrounded, and the
superstitions which are the creed of his age, form
the poet's mind. Rocks, mountains, seas, unsubdued forests, unnavigable rivers, surround him
with forms of power and mystery, which ignorance
and fear have peopled with spirits, under multi-
farious names of gods, goddesses, nymphs, genii,
and dæmons. Of all these personages marvellous
tales are in existence : the nymphs are not indifferent to handsome young men, and the gentle-
men-genii are much troubled and very troublesome
with a propensity to be rude to pretty maidens :

the bard, therefore, finds no difficulty in tracing the genealogy of his chief to any of the deities in his neighbourhood with whom the said chief may be most desirous of claiming relationship.

In this pursuit, as in all others, some, of course, will attain a very marked pre-eminence ; and these will be held in high honour, like Demodocus in the Odyssey, and will be consequently inflated with boundless vanity, like Thamyris in the Iliad. Poets are as yet the only historians and chroniclers of their time, and the sole depositories of all the knowledge of their age ; and though this knowledge is rather a crude congeries of traditional phantasies than a collection of useful truths, yet, such as it is, they have it to themselves. They are observing and thinking, while others are robbing and fighting: and though their object be nothing more than to secure a share of the spoil, yet they accomplish this end by intellectual, not by physical power : their success excites emulation to the attainment of intellectual eminence : thus they sharpen their own wits and awaken those of others, at the same time that they gratify vanity and amuse curiosity. A skilful display of the little knowledge they have gains them credit for the possession of much more which they have not. Their familiarity with the secret history of gods and genii obtains for them, without much difficulty, the reputation of inspiration ; thus they are not only historians, but theologians, moralists, and legislators : delivering their oracles *ex cathedrâ*, and being indeed often themselves (as Orpheus and Amphion) regarded as portions and emanations of divinity : building cities with a song, and leading brutes with a symphony ; which are only metaphors for the faculty of leading multitudes by the nose.

The golden age of poetry finds its materials in the age of iron. This age begins when poetry begins to be retrospective ; when something like a more extended system of civil polity is established, when personal strength and courage avail less to the aggrandizing of their possessor, and to the making and marring of kings and kingdoms, and are checked by organised bodies, social institutions, and hereditary successions. Men also live more in the light of truth and within the interchange of observation ; and thus perceive that the agency of gods and genii is not so frequent among themselves as, to judge from the songs and legends of the past time, it was among their ancestors. From these two circumstances, really diminished personal power, and apparently diminished familiarity with gods and genii, they very easily and naturally deduce two conclusions : 1st, That men are degenerated, and 2nd, That they are less in favour with the gods. The people of the petty states and colonies, which have now acquired stability and form, which owed their origin and first prosperity to the talents and courage of a single chief, magnify their founder through the mists of distance and tradition, and perceive him achieving wonders with a god or goddess always at his elbow. They find his name and his exploits thus magnified and accompanied in their traditionary songs, which are their only memorials. All that is said of him is in this character. There is nothing to contradict it. The man and his exploits and his tutelary deities are mixed and blended in one invariable association. The marvellous, too, is very much like a snow-ball : it grows as it rolls downward, till the little nucleus of truth, which began its descent from the summit, is hidden in the accumulation of superinduced hyperbole.

When tradition, thus adorned and exaggerated, has surrounded the founders of families and states with so much adventitious power and magnificence, there is no praise which a living poet can, without fear of being kicked for clumsy flattery, address to a living chief, that will not still leave the impression that the latter is not so great a man as his ancestors. The man must, in this case, be praised through his ancestors. Their greatness must be established, and he must be shown to be their worthy descendant. All the people of a state are interested in the founder of their state. All states that have harmonised into a common form of society, are interested in their respective founders. All men are interested in their ancestors. All men love to look back into the days that are past. In these circumstances traditional national poetry is reconstructed and brought, like chaos, into order and form. The interest is more universal : under-

standing is enlarged : passion still has scope and
play : character is still various and strong : nature
is still unsubdued and existing in all her beauty
and magnificence, and men are not yet excluded
from her observation by the magnitude of cities,
or the daily confinement of civic life : poetry is
more an art : it requires greater skill in numbers,
greater command of language, more extensive and
various knowledge, and greater comprehensiveness
of mind.   It still exists without rivals in any other
department of literature ; and even the arts, painting and sculpture certainly, and music probably,
are comparatively rude and imperfect.   The whole
field of intellect is its own.   It has no rivals in
history, nor in philosophy, nor in science.   It is
cultivated by the greatest intellects of the age, and
listened to by all the rest.   This is the age of
Homer, the golden age of poetry.   Poetry has now
attained its perfection : it has attained the point
which it cannot pass : genius therefore seeks new
forms for the treatment of the same subjects :
hence the lyric poetry of Pindar and Alcæus, and
the tragic poetry of Æschylus and Sophocles.
The favour of kings, the honour of the Olympic
crown, the applause of present multitudes, all that
can feed vanity and stimulate rivalry, await the
successful cultivator of this art, till its forms become
exhausted, and new rivals arise around it in new
fields of literature, which gradually acquire more
influence as, with the progress of reason and
civilisation, facts become more interesting than

fiction : indeed, the maturity of poetry may be considered the infancy of history. The transition from Homer to Herodotus is scarcely more remarkable than that from Herodotus to Thucydides : in the gradual dereliction of fabulous incident and ornamented language. Herodotus is as much a poet, in relation to Thucydides, as Homer is in relation to Herodotus. The history of Herodotus is half a poem : it was written while the whole field of literature yet belonged to the Muses, and the nine books of which it was composed were therefore of right, as well of courtesy, superinscribed with their nine names.

Speculations, too, and disputes, on the nature of man and of mind ; on moral duties and on good and evil ; on the animate and inanimate components of the visible world ; begin to share attention with the eggs of Leda and the horns of Io, and to draw off from poetry a portion of its once undivided audience.

Then comes the silver age, or the poetry of civilised life. This poetry is of two kinds, imitative and original. The imitative consists in recasting, and giving an exquisite polish to the poetry of the age of gold : of this Virgil is the most obvious and striking example. The original is chiefly comic, didactic, or satiric : as in Menander, Aristophanes, Horace, and Juvenal. The poetry of this age is characterised by an exquisite and fastidious selection of words, and a laboured and somewhat monotonous harmony of expression :

but its monotony consists in this, that experience
having exhausted all the varieties of modulation,
the civilised poetry selects the most beautiful, and
prefers the repetition of these to ranging through
the variety of all. But the best expression being
that into which the idea naturally falls, it requires
the utmost labour and care so to reconcile the in-
flexibility of civilised language and the laboured
polish of versification with the idea intended to be
expressed, that sense may not appear to be sacri-
ficed to sound. Hence numerous efforts and rare
success.

This state of poetry is, however, a step towards
its extinction. Feeling and passion are best painted
in, and roused by, ornamental and figurative language; but the reason and the understanding are
best addressed in the simplest and most unvar-
nished phrase. Pure reason and dispassionate
truth would be perfectly ridiculous in verse, as we
may judge by versifying one of Euclid's demonstra-
tions. This will be found true of all dispassionate
reasoning whatever, and of all reasoning that requires comprehensive views and enlarged combinations. It is only the more tangible points of
morality, those which command assent at once,
those which have a mirror in every mind, and in
which the severity of reason is warmed and rendered palatable by being mixed up with feeling and
imagination, that are applicable even to what is
called moral poetry : and as the sciences of morals
and of mind advance towards perfection, as they

become more enlarged and comprehensive in their views, as reason gains the ascendancy in them over imagination and feeling, poetry can no longer accompany them in their progress, but drops into the background, and leaves them to advance alone.

Thus the empire of thought is withdrawn from poetry, as the empire of facts had been before. In respect of the latter, the poet of the age of iron celebrates the achievements of his contemporaries ; the poet of the age of gold celebrates the heroes of the age of iron ; the poet of the age of silver re-casts the poems of the age of gold : we may here see how very light a ray of historical truth is sufficient to dissipate all the illusions of poetry. We know no more of the men than of the gods of the Iliad ; no more of Achilles than we do of Thetis ; no more of Hector and Andromache than we do of Vulcan and Venus : these belong altogether to poetry ; history has no share in them ; but Virgil knew better than to write an epic about Cæsar ; he left him to Livy ; and travelled out of the confines of truth and history into the old regions of poetry and fiction.

Good sense and elegant learning, conveyed in polished and somewhat monotonous verse, are the perfection of the original and imitative poetry of civilised life. Its range is limited, and when exhausted, nothing remains but the *crambe repetita* of commonplace, which at length becomes thoroughly wearisome, even to the most indefatigable readers of the newest new nothings.

It is now evident that poetry must either cease to be cultivated, or strike into a new path. The poets of the age of gold have been imitated and repeated till no new imitation will attract notice : the limited range of ethical and didactic poetry is exhausted : the associations of daily life in an advanced stute of society are of very dry, methodical, un-poetical matter-of-fact : but there is always a multitude of listless idlers, yawning for amusement, and gaping for novelty : and the poet makes it his glory to be foremost among their purveyors.

Then comes the age of brass, which, by rejecting the polish and the learning of the age of silver, and taking a retrograde strike to the barbarisms and crude traditions of the age of iron, professes to return to nature and revive the age of gold. This is the second childhood of poetry. For the comprehensive energy of the Homeric Muse, which, by giving at once the grand outline of things, presented to the mind a vivid picture in one or two verses, inimitable alike in simplicity and magnificence, is substituted a verbose and minutely-detailed description of thoughts, passions, actions, persons, and things, in that loose rambling style of verse, which any one may write, *stans pede in uno*, at the rate of two hundred lines in an hour. To this age may be referred all the poets who flourished in the decline of the Roman Empire. The best specimen of it, though not the most generally known, is the Dionysiaca of Nonnus, which con-

tains many passages of exceeding beauty in the
midst of masses of amplification and repetition.

The iron age of classical poetry may be called
the barbaric of the golden, the Homeric; the silver,
the Virgilian; and the brass, the Nonnic.

Modern poetry has also its four ages: but "it
wears its rue with a difference."

To the age of brass in the ancient world succeeded the dark ages, in which the light of the
Gospel began to spread over Europe, and in which,
by a mysterious and inscrutable dispensation, the
darkness thickened with the progress of the light.
The tribes that overran the Roman Empire brought
back the days of barbarism, but with this difference, that there were many books in the world,
many places in which they were preserved, and
occasionally some one by whom they were read,
who indeed (if he escaped being burned *pour l'amour
de Dieu*) generally lived an object of mysterious fear,
with the reputation of magician, alchymist, and astrologer. The emerging of the nations of Europe
from this superinduced barbarism, and their settling
into new forms of polity, was accompanied, as the
first ages of Greece had been, with a wild spirit of
adventure, which, co-operating with new manners
and new superstitions, raised up a fresh crop of
chimæras, not less fruitful, though far less beautiful, than those of Greece. The semi-deification
of women by the maxims of the age of chivalry,
combining with these new fables, produced the
romance of the middle ages. The founders of the

new line of heroes took the place of the demi-gods
of Grecian poetry. Charlemagne and his Paladins,
Arthur and his knights of the round table, the
heroes of the iron age of chivalrous poetry, were
seen through the same magnifying mist of distance,
and their exploits were celebrated with even more
extravagant hyperbole. These legends, combined
with the exaggerated love that pervades the songs
of the troubadours, the reputation of magic that
attached to learned men, the infant wonders of
natural philosophy, the crazy fanaticism of the
crusades, the power and privileges of the great
feudal chiefs, and the holy mysteries of monks and
nuns, formed a state of society in which no two
laymen could meet without fighting, and in which
the three staple ingredients of lover, prize-fighter,
and fanatic, that composed the basis of the character of every true man, were mixed up and diversified, in different individuals and classes, with so
many distinctive excellencies, and under such an
infinite motley variety of costume, as gave the range
of a most extensive and picturesque field to the
two great constituents of poetry, love and battle.

From these ingredients of the iron age of modern
poetry, dispersed in the rhymes of minstrels and
the songs of the troubadours, arose the golden age,
in which the scattered materials were harmonised
and blended about the time of the revival of learning; but with this peculiar difference, that Greek
and Roman literature pervaded all the poetry of
the golden age of modern poetry, and hence re-

sulted a heterogeneous compound of all ages and nations in one picture; an infinite licence, which gave to the poet the free range of the whole field of imagination and memory. This was carried very far by Ariosto, but farthest of all by Shakespeare and his contemporaries, who used time and locality merely because they could not do without them, because every action must have its when and where; but they made no scruple of deposing a Roman Emperor by an Italian Count, and sending him off in the disguise of a French pilgrim to be shot with a blunderbuss by an English archer. This makes the Old English drama very picturesque, at any rate, in the variety of costume, and very diversified in action and character: though it is a picture of nothing that ever was seen on earth except a Venetian carnival.

The greatest of English poets, Milton, may be said to stand alone between the ages of gold and silver, combining the excellencies of both; for with all the energy, and power, and freshness of the first, he united all the studied and elaborate magnificence of the second.

The silver age succeeded; beginning with Dryden, coming to perfection with Pope, and ending with Goldsmith, Collins, and Gray.

Cowper divested verse of its exquisite polish; he thought in metre, but paid more attention to his thoughts than his verse. It would be difficult to draw the boundary of prose and blank verse between his letters and his poetry.

The silver age was the reign of authority ; but
authority now began to be shaken, not only in
poetry but in the whole sphere of its dominion.
The contemporaries of Gray and Cowper were
deep and elaborate thinkers. The subtle scepti-
cism of Hume, the solemn irony of Gibbon, the
daring paradoxes of Rousseau, and the biting
ridicule of Voltaire, directed the energies of four
extraordinary minds to shape every portion of
the reign of authority. Inquiry was roused, the
activity of intellect was excited, and poetry came
in for its share of the general result. The
changes had been rung on lovely maid and
sylvan shade, summer heat and green retreat,
waving trees and sighing breeze, gentle swains
and amorous pains, by versifiers who took them
on trust, as meaning something very soft and
tender, without much caring what : but with this
general activity of intellect came a necessity for
even poets to appear to know something of what
they professed to talk of. Thomson and Cowper
looked at the trees and hills which so many ingenious gentlemen had rhymed about so long without
looking at them at all, and the effect of the operation on poetry was like the discovery of a new
world. Painting shared the influence, and the
principles of picturesque beauty were explored by
adventurous essayists with indefatigable pertina-
city. The success which attended these experi-
ments, and the pleasure which resulted from them,
had the usual effect of all new enthusiasms, that

of turning the heads of a few unfortunate persons, the patriarchs of the age of brass, who, mistaking the prominent novelty for the all-important totality, seem to have ratiocinated much in the following manner : " Poetical genius is the finest of all things, and we feel that we have more of it than any one ever had. The way to bring it to perfection is to cultivate poetical impressions exclusively. Poetical impressions can be received only among natural scenes : for all that is artificial is anti-poetical. Society is artificial, therefore we will live out of society. The mountains are natural, therefore we will live in the mountains. There we shall be shining models of purity and virtue, passing the whole day in the innocent and amiable occupation of going up and down hill, receiving poetical impressions, and communicating them in immortal verse to admiring generations." To some such perversion of intellect we owe that egregious confraternity of rhymesters, known by the name of the Lake Poets; who certainly did receive and communicate to the world some of the most extraordinary poetical impressions that ever were heard of, and ripened into models of public virtue, too splendid to need illustration. They wrote verses on a new principle ; saw rocks and rivers in a new light ; and remaining studiously ignorant of history, society, and human nature, cultivated the phantasy only at the expense of the memory and the reason ; and contrived, though they had retreated from the world for the express purpose of seeing Nature as she

was, to see her only as she was not, converting the
land they lived in into a sort of fairy-land, which
they peopled with mysticisms and chimæras. This
gave what is called a new tone to poetry, and conjured up a herd of desperate imitators, who have
brought the age of brass prematurely to its dotage.

The descriptive poetry of the present day has
been called by its cultivators a return to nature.
Nothing is more impertinent than this pretension.
Poetry cannot travel out of the regions of its birth,
the uncultivated lands of semi-civilised men. Mr
Wordsworth, the great leader of the returners to
nature, cannot describe a scene under his own
eyes without putting into it the shadow of a Danish
boy or the living ghost of Lucy Gray, or some
similar phantastical parturition of the moods of
his own mind.

In the origin and perfection of poetry, all the
associations of life were composed of poetical
materials. With us it is decidedly the reverse.
We know, too, that there are no Dryads in Hyde-
park nor Naiads in the Regent's-canal. But barbaric manners and supernatural interventions are
essential to poetry. Either in the scene, or in the
time, or in both, it must be remote from our
ordinary perceptions. While the historian and the
philosopher are advancing in, and accelerating,
the progress of knowledge, the poet is wallowing
in the rubbish of departed ignorance, and raking
up the ashes of dead savages to find gewgaws and
rattles for the grown babies of the age. Mr Scott

digs up the poachers and cattle-stealers of the ancient border. Lord Byron cruises for thieves and pirates on the shores of the Morea and among the Greek islands. Mr Southey wades through ponderous volumes of travels and old chronicles, from which he carefully selects all that is false, useless, and absurd, as being essentially poetical ; and when he has a commonplace book full of monstrosities, strings them into an epic. Mr Wordsworth picks up village legends from old women and sextons ; and Mr Coleridge, to the valuable information acquired from similar sources, superadds the dreams of crazy theologians and the mysticisms of German metaphysics, and favours the world with visions in verse, in which the quadruple elements of sexton, old woman, Jeremy Taylor, and Emanuel Kant are harmonised into a delicious poetical compound. Mr Moore presents us with a Persian, and Mr Campbell with a Pennsylvanian tale, both formed on the same principle as Mr Southey's epics, by extracting from a perfunctory and desultory perusal of a collection of voyages and travels all that useful investigation would not seek for and that common sense would reject.

These disjointed relics of tradition and fragments of second-hand observation, being woven into a tissue of verse, constructed on what Mr Coleridge calls a new principle (that is, no principle at all), compose a modern-antique compound of frippery and barbarism, in which the puling

E

sentimentality of the present time is grafted on the
misrepresented ruggedness of the past into a
heterogeneous congeries of unamalgamating manners, sufficient to impose on the common readers
of poetry, over whose understandings the poet of
this class possesses that commanding advantage,
which, in all circumstances and conditions of life,
a man who knows something, however little, always
possesses over one who knows nothing.

A poet in our times is a semi-barbarian in a
civilised community. He lives in the days that
are past. His ideas, thoughts, feelings, associations, are all with barbarous manners, obsolete
customs, and exploded superstitions. The march
of his intellect is like that of a crab, backward.
The brighter the light diffused around him by the
progress of reason, the thicker is the darkness of
antiquated barbarism, in which he buries himself
like a mole, to throw up the barren hillocks of his
Cimmerian labours. The philosophic mental tranquillity which looks round with an equal eye on all
external things, collects a store of ideas, discrimi-
nates their relative value, assigns to all their proper
place, and from the materials of useful knowledge
thus collected, appreciated, and arranged, forms
new combinations that impress the stamp of their
power and utility on the real business of life, is
diametrically the reverse of that frame of mind
which poetry inspires, or from which poetry can
emanate. The highest inspirations of poetry are
resolvable into three ingredients: the rant of un-

regulated passion, the whining of exaggerated feeling, and the cant of factitious sentiment : and can therefore serve only to ripen a splendid lunatic like Alexander, a puling driveller like Werter, or a morbid dreamer like Wordsworth. It can never make a philosopher, nor a statesman, nor in any class of life an useful or rational man. It cannot claim the slightest share in any one of the comforts and utilities of life of which we have witnessed so many and so rapid advances. But though not useful, it may be said it is highly ornamental, and deserves to be cultivated for the pleasure it yields. Even if this be granted, it does not follow that a writer of poetry in the present state of society is not a waster of his own time, and a robber of that of others. Poetry is not one of those arts which, like painting, require repetition and multiplication, in order to be diffused among society. There are more good poems already existing than are sufficient to employ that portion of life which any mere reader and recipient of poetical impressions should devote to them, and these having been produced in poetical times, are far superior in all the characteristics of poetry to the artificial reconstructions of a few morbid ascetics in unpoetical times. To read the promiscuous rubbish of the present time to the exclusion of the select treasures of the past, is to substitute the worse for the better variety of the same mode of enjoyment.

But in whatever degree poetry is cultivated, it must necessarily be to the neglect of some branch of useful study : and it is a lamentable spectacle to see minds, capable of better things, running to seed in the specious indolence of these empty aimless mockeries of intellectual exertion. Poetry was the mental rattle that awakened the attention of intellect in the infancy of civil society : but for the maturity of mind to make a serious business of the playthings of its childhood, is as absurd as for a full-grown man to rub his gums with coral, and cry to be charmed to sleep by the jingle of silver bells.

As to that small portion of our contemporary poetry, which is neither descriptive, nor narrative, nor dramatic, and which, for want of a better name, may be called ethical, the most distinguished portion of it, consisting merely of querulous, egotistical rhapsodies, to express the writer's high dissatisfaction with the world and everything in it, serves only to confirm what has been said of the semi-barbarous character of poets, who from singing dithyrambics and " Io Triumphe," while society was savage, grow rabid, and out of their element as it becomes polished and enlightened.

Now, when we consider that it is not to the thinking and studious, and scientific and philosophical part of the community, not to those whose minds are bent on the pursuit and promotion of permanently useful ends and aims, that poets must address their minstrelsy, but to that much larger portion of the reading public, whose minds are not awakened to the desire of valuable knowledge, and who are indifferent to anything beyond being charmed, moved, excited, affected, and exalted: charmed by harmony, moved by sentiment, excited by passion, affected by pathos, and exalted by sublimity: harmony, which is language on the rack of Procrustes; sentiment, which is canting egotism in the mask of refined feeling; passion, which is the commotion of a weak and selfish mind; pathos, which is the whining of an unmanly spirit; and sublimity, which is the inflation of an empty head: when we consider that the great and permanent interests of human society become more and more the main-spring of intellectual pursuit; that in proportion as they become so, the subordinacy of the ornamental to the useful will be more and more seen and acknowledged; and that therefore the progress of useful art and science, and of moral and political knowledge, will continue more and more to withdraw attention from frivolous and unconducive, to solid and conducive studies: that therefore the poetical audience will not only continually diminish in the proportion of its number to that of the rest of the reading public, but will also sink lower and lower in the comparison of intellectual acquirement: when we consider that the poet must still please his audience, and must therefore continue to sink to their level, while the rest of the community is rising above it: we may easily conceive that the day is not distant, when the degraded state of every species of poetry will be as generally recognised as

that of dramatic poetry has long been : and this
not from any decrease either of intellectual power,
or intellectual acquisition, but because intellectual
power and intellectual acquisition have turned
themselves into other and better channels, and
have abandoned the cultivation and the fate of
poetry to the degenerate fry of modern rhymesters,
and their olympic judges, the magazine critics,
who continue to debate and promulgate oracles
about poetry, as if it were still what it was in the
Homeric age, the all-in-all of intellectual progres-
sion, and as if there were no such things in existence as mathematicians, astronomers, chemists,
moralists, metaphysicians, historians, politicians,
and political economists, who have built into the
upper air of intelligence a pyramid, from the
summit of which they see the modern Parnassus
far beneath them, and, knowing how small a place
it occupies in the comprehensiveness of their
prospect, smile at the little ambition and the cir-
cumscribed perceptions with which the drivellers
and mountebanks upon it are contending for the
poetical palm and the critical chair.   ·

HORÆ DRAMATICÆ.

No. I.

[Published in *Fraser's Magazine*, 1852, vol. xlv. No. cclxvii.]

OETHE, we think—for we cannot cite chapter and verse—says somewhere something to this effect—that the realities of life present little that is either satisfactory or hopeful; and that the only refuge for a mind which aspires to better views of society, is in the idealities of the theatre.

Without going to the full extent of this opinion, we may say, that the drama has been the favourite study of this portion of our plurality, and has furnished to us, on many and many occasions, a refuge of light and tranquillity from the storms and darkness of every-day life.

It is needless to look further than to the Athenian theatre and Shakspeare, to establish the position that the drama has combined the highest poetry with the highest wisdom; neither is it necessary to show that the great masters of the art have a long train of worthy followers, partially familiar to all who look to dramatic literature for

amusement alone, and more extensively as to those
who make it a subject of study.

Still there are many excellent dramas comparatively little known ; much valuable matter bearing
on the drama, remaining to be developed ; and
many dramatic questions, which continue to be
subjects of controversy, and offer topics of interesting discussion.

It is our purpose to present our views of some
of these subjects, in the form of analyses or criti-
cisms ; not following any order of chronology or
classification, but only that in which our readings
or reminiscences may suggest them.

QUEROLUS ; or, THE BURIED TREASURE.

A ROMAN COMEDY OF THE THIRD CENTURY.

This comedy, which, from internal evidence, is
assignable to the age of Diocletian and Maximian,
is the only Roman comedy which, in addition to
the remains of Plautus and Terence, has escaped
the ravages of time.   It is not only on this
account a great literary curiosity, but it is in itself
a very amusing and original drama.   It is little
known in this country.

The first editors of this comedy had access to
several manuscript copies of it.   The last editor
had access to two : the Codex Vossianus, now in
the library at Leyden, in the margin of which

Vossius had written the various readings of another, the Codex Pithœi; and the Codex Parisinus, now in the library at Paris, a manuscript apparently of the eleventh century.

The first printed edition was edited by P. Danielis, in 1564. The second edition was edited by Rittershusius, and printed by Commelinus, in 1595. The third edition was published by Pareus, at the end of his edition of Plautus, in 1619. The fourth and last edition is that of Klinkhämer, published at Amsterdam in 1829. Of these editions, the first, third, and fourth are in the British Museum; the second and fourth are in our possession.*

We have thus had the opportunity of consulting all the editions of the work. The first edition was inaccessible to Klinkhämer. The second edition contains all that is important in the first, with much that is not in any other; including a long poem by Vitalis Blesensis, a writer of the middle ages, in which the story is narrated in elegiac verse: the author professing, that he now does for a second comedy of Plautus what he had previously done for his *Amphitryon.* The author of the comedy is, however, as we shall subsequently notice, innocent of its ascription to Plautus.

In the first three editions, the text was printed as

* The play has since been edited by Peiper, 1575, and very elaborately and with a French prose translation by Havet, in the Bibliothèque de l' École des Hautes Études. Paris, 1880-1.—G.

prose. Klinkämer recognised the traces of metre, and arranged the whole into verse, printing the prose text on the left-hand pages, and the metrical arrangement on the right. The task is executed with much skill, and little arbitrary change. In this portion of his work, as indeed in the whole of it, he derived great advantage from having been the pupil of D. J. Van Lennep,* at whose instigation he undertook the edition. The result is, a most agreeable reading, of which we regretted to come to the close.

This play is called *Querolus, sive Aulularia—* "Querolus, or the Comedy of the *Aula,* or *Olla,*" a large covered pot or vessel of any kind, which is in this case the depository of a treasure. The dramatis personæ are—

LAR FAMILIARIS.	SYCOPHANTA.
QUEROLUS.	PANTOLABUS.†
MANDROGERUS.	ARBITER.
SARDANAPALUS.	

Plautus's comedy of *Aulularia* (the basis of

* The learned and accomplished editor of *Terentianus Maurus.* He completed the edition which Santenius had begun.

† The MSS. and editions have all "Pantomalus," a barbarous composite, suitable, no doubt, to the age, but not to so correct and elegant a writer as the author of this comedy. " Pantolabus " is classical (see Hor. *Sat.* i. 8, 11) ; and *Take-all* suits the character in question better than *All-bad.* [This very ingenious emendation is not noticed by subsequent editors, who seem to be unacquainted with Peacock's essay. —G.]

Molière's *L'Avare*) takes its name from a similar subject ; but there is nothing in common between the comedies, excepting the buried treasure, the title, and the circumstances of the prologue being spoken by the household deity, the Lar Familiaris.

In Plautus's prologue, the Lar tells the audience, that the heads of the families had been a succession of misers, one of whom had buried a treasure, the secret of which he had not the heart, even when dying, to reveal to his son ; that the son had lived and died poor and parsimonious, and had shown no honour to him, the Lar ; in consequence of which he had done nothing towards aiding him to discover the buried treasure : that the grandson, the present *pater familias*, was no better than his predecessors ; but that he had a daughter who was very pious towards her household deity ; on which account he had led the father to the discovery of the treasure, in order that the daughter might have a dowry.

The comedy of *Querolus* has no female character, and the hero does not appear to have a family. The Lar tells the audience, that Euclio, the father of Querolus, going abroad on business, had buried a treasure before the domestic altar ; that, dying abroad, he had entrusted the secret to Mandrogerus, and had given him a letter to Querolus, enjoining his son to divide the treasure with his friend Mandrogerus, as a reward for faithfully delivering the message ; that Mandrogerus had made a scheme for getting surreptitious possession of the whole; that he, the Lar, would frustrate this scheme, and take care that the treasure should go to its right owner, whom he describes as not bad, but ungrateful.

The first scene consists of a dialogue between Querolus and the Lar. Querolus enters, complaining of Fortune, when the Lar presents himself before him.

Quer. Oh, Fortune !—oh, blind Fortune ! impious Fate !
Lar. Hail, Querolus !
Quer. What wouldst thou with me, friend ?
I owe thee nothing, nor have stolen goods
Of thine in my possession.
Lar. Be not angry.
Stay ; I must talk with thee.
Quer. I have no leisure.
Lar. Stay, for thou must. 'Tis I, whom thou hast called
In terms of accusation.
Quer. I accused
Fortune and Fate.
Lar. I am thy household god,
Whom thou call'st Fate and Fortune.
Quer. It is strange.
I know not what to think ; but this appears
One of the Genii or the Mysteries.
His robe is white, and radiance is around him.
Lar. Though thy complaint is baseless, Querolus,
I am moved by it, and have come to render,
What never Lar to mortal did before,
The reason of thy state. Now, tell thy grievances.
Quer. The day would not be long enough.
Lar. Well, briefly :
A few ; the heaviest.
Quer. One only question
Resolve me : wherefore do the unjust thrive,
And the just suffer ?

The Lar proceeds to interrogate Querolus, as to his right to include himself in the latter class ; and having led him to confess himself guilty of robbing orchards as a boy, of perjuring himself as a lover, of intriguing with his neighbour's wife as a man, and of sundry other peccadilloes, which society tolerates and justice condemns, he concludes that he has no right to look on himself as an egregious specimen of injured virtue.

Querolus, nevertheless, insists that much worse men are much better off. He has suffered by a false friend ; his father has left him nothing but his poor house and land ; he has a slave, Pantolabus, who does nothing but eat and drink enormously ; his last crops were destroyed by a storm ; he has a bad neighbour. To all which the Lar answers : Many fathers have not even left either house or land : others have had many false friends, many drunken slaves, many bad neighbours : he is well enough with only one of each. Querolus specifies somebody who abounds in worldly comforts. But, says the Lar, he has an incurable malady. How is your own health ? Querolus is quite well. The Lar asks, Would you change conditions? Is not health the first of blessings ? Querolus admits that he is the best off of the two; but still insists that, though positively it is well with him, it is ill, comparatively with others. The Lar then gives him his choice of conditions. Querolus first desires military glory ; then civil honours. The difficulties and troubles of both being shown, he rejects both, and desires a private life of affluence, in which his riches may give him sufficient authority to domineer over his neighbours. The Lar tells him, that if he wishes to live where public law has no authority, he had better go to the Loire, where every man is judge in his own cause, and the stronger writes his decrees with a cudgel on the bones and skin of the weaker.

This passage, Klinkhämer is of opinion, relates to the *Bagaudæ*, who, about the end of the reign of Diocletian, established in that portion of Gaul one of the earliest combinations of Socialism and Lynch law : not without dreadful provocation from the cruelties and extortions of the Roman rulers : and were with difficulty reduced to submission, after a war of some years, by the Emperor Maximian.* The history of this Bagaudic war may be read in Gibbon, chap. xiii. Querolus, not without a sarcastic reflection on the innocence and happiness of sylvan life, renounces the offered share in this forest republic : goes through a series of wishes for different states of life, each of which, with the conditions attached to it, he successively rejects : then comes to persons, whose position he would like to occupy.

* Other editors assign the Querolus to the early part of the fifth century, identifying the Rutilius, to whom it is dedicated, with the poet Claudius Rutilius Numatianus, and pointing out that the Bagaudæ continued to be more or less troublesome for two hundred years. The mention of the solidus, first coined by Constantine, seems a conclusive argument against Klinkhämer's date.—G.

Quer. Give me at least the money-chests of Titius.
Lar. Yes, with his gout.
Quer.   No gout.
Lar.   Nor money-chests.
Quer. Why, give me, then, the troop of dancing-girls,
Which the new-come old usurer has brought with
    him.
Lar. Take the whole chorus : take Cytheris, Paphia,
Briseis : with the weight of Nestor's years.
Quer. Ha ! ha ! and wherefore ?
Lar.   The old usurer has it.
The years and dancing-girls must go together.
Quer. This will not do. Well, give me impudence.*
Lar. Be impudent, and dominate the forum :
But with the loss of wisdom.
Quer.   Why ?
Lar.   The impudent
Are never wise.
Quer.   Why, then, are no men happy ?
Lar. Some are : not those you think so.
Quer.   If I show you
One rich and healthy too, is he not happy ?
Lar. You see the healthy body : not the mind :
That may be sick with envy, hope, or fear,
Ambition, avarice unsatisfied.
The face shows not the heart. What if, in public
Joyous, he mourns at home ? Loves not his wife ?
Or loves too much, and dies with jealousy ?

Querolus gives up the discussion, and leaves his
fate to his Lar. The Lar tells him, he shall be
rich in spite of himself; he shall do all in his
power to send away his good luck, but it shall

* Querolus seems to have thought with Butler :
    " He that has but impudence
    To all things has a just pretence."

force itself upon him : with several other ambigui-
ties of prophecy, over which he leaves Querolus
marvelling. Querolus, after a soliloquy, in which
he expresses his perplexity, goes on.

Mandrogerus enters, with Sycophanta and Sardanapalus. Mandrogerus has laid a scheme for
getting possession of the buried treasure, without
giving any portion of it to Querolus, and has
selected the other two knaves as his instruments.

Mandrogerus exults in his anticipated success.
But Sycophanta has had a dream of bad omen :

Syc.   I saw last night the treasure, which we hope
          To get into our hands.
Mand.   What then ?
Syc.   I saw
          Pieces of gold : but only as a glimpse,
          Through barbed hooks and rings, and little chains.
Mand. Didst thou not dream of fetters too, and lashes?
Sard.   Oh, inauspicious dreamer ! I explode thee,
          And thy ill omens. I had my dream too :
          'Twas of a funeral.
Mand.   The gods prosper thee !
Sard.   We paid the last rites to I know not whom.
Mand. 'Tis well.
Sard.   And wept the dead, although a stranger.
Mand. These are good signs : dreams go by contraries :
          Funerals show joy : and tears belong to laughter.
          I also had my dream. I know not who
          Told me, the fates assigned to none but me,
          To find the buried gold : but it should profit me,
          Only so much as I might swallow from it.
Syc.   Most admirable dream ! What other use
          Can we have for it, but to eat and drink it ?

They proceed to reconnoitre the locality, according to the indications received from Euclio : a little temple : a silversmith's shop : a lofty house with oaken doors. They remark that the upright bars are wide apart, and not defended with tenter-hooks ; showing an inhabitant who has nothing to fear from thieves. Mandrogerus then inquires, if they exactly remember the description of the interior. They repeat it accordingly. The portico on the right hand of the entrance. Three little images in the *sacrarium.** An altar in the middle. The gold before the altar. So far all is right. They thoroughly understand their parts. The business of Mandrogerus is to divine. That of the other two is to lie. Mandrogerus goes out to abide his time. His accomplices watch the coming of Querolus, who enters well-disposed, by his previous interview with the Lar, to credulity in supernatural matters. They stand aside, pretending not to see him, and talking as if they did not mean to be heard. He catches some sounds which induce him to listen.

Sard. I have known magi and astrologers ;
But never one like this. Soon as he sees you,
He calls you by your name : expounds your parents,
Slaves, family : the history of your life :
All you have done, and will do.

Quer. (*apart.*)   This must be
A man worth seeing.

* *Sacrarium* here signifies a place set apart to sacred purposes in a private dwelling. The nearest corresponding modern term is *oratory.*

F

Sard.   Let us lose no time
    In seeking him.
Syc.   I would most willingly ;
    But, at this moment, I have not the leisure.
Quer. I would fain seek him too.   Hail, friends.
Syc.   We answer
    Thy friendly salutation.
Quer.   Is your talk
    Of secrets ?
Sard.   Secrets to the general ;
    Not to the wise.
Quer.   I seemed to catch a mention
    Of some great magus.
Sard.   One most wonderful
    In divination.   Who, or whence, I know not.
Quer. Is he so deep in art ?
Sard.   Most absolute :
    Wherefore, I pray you, Sycophanta, come
    Straightway to visit him.
Syc.   I have friends at home,
    Awaiting me on urgent business.

Sardanapalus over-rules Sycophanta's objections.
Querolus entreats to be of their party.   They make
many difficulties, and at last consent.   Sycophanta
suggests to Sardanapalus, that the astrologer may
be an impostor ; and, anticipating all the scruples
that Querolus might have raised, completes the
conquest of his confidence.   While they are discussing, Mandrogerus most opportunely comes in
sight, walking slowly onward, in profound medita-
tion.   They stop him, and respectfully request to
be permitted to consult him, and imbibe some
portion of his wisdom.   He answers, like one over-
flowing with it, and most bountiful in its distribu-

tion, that he is at leisure, and will answer any questions they please to ask.

They begin with questions, respecting the powers to be propitiated; the offerings to be made to them; the secondary instruments through which they deliver their oracles: stars; celestial and terrestrial prodigies; consecrated animals; harpies, geese, and cynocephali: a very curious enumeration of powers, never otherwise than malevolently exerted, unless under the influence of abundant gifts and sacrifices, though it is not the god himself who exacts them, but his door-keeper: in all which, while popular superstitions are obviously and ostensibly, Klinkhämer thinks the corruptions and oppressions of the several authorities of the state are covertly satirised.

Sycophanta receives this exposition as thoroughly discouraging all application to the powers in question; and solicits an explanation of some more simple method of solving the mysteries of destiny.

Mand. First, much depends upon the natal hour,
    Whether a man be born to a good fate:
    Next, by propitiation of the Genii,
    Who govern Fate's decrees, to make that good
    Which at the first was ill: by their kind power,
    If Evil Fortune dwell within the walls,
    She may be charmed, and bound, and carried forth.
Quer. This were most excellent; but that we may
    With confidence obey you, having told us
    Much that you know, tell something that you know
    not.
Mand. Assuredly, I know none of you three,
    By any previous knowledge.

Sard.   That is certain.

Mand. First, then, to thee.   Thy name is Sardanapalus:
Poor and low-born.

Sard. 'Tis so.

Mand. A poor man's child,
Mocked with a royal name.

Sard.   .   I can't deny it.

Mand. An idler and a glutton : petulant :
Calamitous thyself, and a calamity
To all who know thee.

Sard.   Eh ! Mandrogerus !
I did not ask thee to proclaim my vices.

Mand. I may not lie.   What hast thou more to ask?

Sard. I have heard too much already.   If thou hast
Aught more, reserve it for my private hearing.

Syc. Now to my turn, Mandrogerus : tell my fortune :
So much of it as may be good : no more.

Mand. I must begin from the beginning : Thou
Art Sycophanta, and of noble birth.

Syc. 'Tis true.

Mand.   A worthless subject from the first.

Syc. Alas !

Mand.   Pressed down by wrongs, compassed by perils
From steel, and fire, and water.

Syc.   It would seem
That thou hadst lived with me.

Mand.   Nought of thy own
Is left to thee : but much of other men's.*

Syc. Too much : too much.   Pray favour me no further.
Turn to this worthy man.

Mand.   Step forward, friend :
Thy name is Querolus.

Quer.   'Tis even so.

Mand. What is the hour?   Between the sixth and seventh.

Quer. Nothing escapes him : he propounds his question

---

* *Aes alienum.*   Debt.

And straightway answers it, like a clepsydra.*

Mand. Mars now is trigon.   Saturn looks to Venus.
Jupiter is quadrate.   Mercury is wroth with him.
The sun is round.   The moon is in her spring. †
I have combined thy genealogy,
Querolus.   Evil Fortune presses thee.

Quer. It is too true.

Mand.   Thy father left thee nothing.
Thy friends give nothing.   Thou hast a bad neigh-
bour ;
A worthless slave.

Quer.   'Tis so.

Mand.   IIis name Pantolabus.
Thou hast another slave : his name is Zeta.

Quer. 'Tis manifest.   .

Syc.   Divine astrologer !

Mand. Shall I describe thy house ?   Full well thou knowest
I ne'er was in it.

Quer.   I would gladly hear.

Mand. Entering, the portico is on the right ;
And the sacrarium opposite.

Quer.   Exactly.

Mand. In the sacrarium are three little statues:
One of the household God ; two of the Genii. ‡

Quer. Thou hast proved thy knowledge.   Now produce the
remedy
Of my ill fortune.

Mand.   That is quickly done ;
Without delay or cost.   Is the sacrarium
Secret and solitary?

* *Clepsydra :* a water-clock, by which time was measured,
as by an hour-glass.

† Peacock has evidently not grasped the technical signifi-
cation of *saltu,* any more than the French translator who
renders it *danse.*   The meaning is that the moon is increas-
ing in light.—G.

‡ The *Genius Loci :* and the *Genius Domini.*

Quer.   Even so.

Mand. Nothing concealed there ?

Quer.   Nothing there at all ;
    Except the images.

Mand.   There must be performed
    A solemn rite : but thee and every one
    That rite excludes.

Quer.   So be it.

Mand.   And by strangers
    The rite must be performed.

Quer.   So let it be.

Mand. Could we find any on so short a notice :—
    'Twere well and opportune, if these would aid us.

The two knaves, on the invitation of Querolus,
very obligingly promise their assistance : and
Querolus desires Pantolabus to run for his friend
and neighbour, the Arbiter.* Mandrogerus, who
does not like this sort of witness, urges Querolus
not to delay. The hour is auspicious. The com-
bination of stars is most promising. Mandrogerus
asks Querolus if he has an empty box. Querolus
replies, he is too well provided with empty boxes.
One will be necessary, says Mandrogerus, to carry
out the *lustrum.†* And they go in to perform
their ceremonies.

The next scene brings in Pantolabus, who in-

* *Arbiter.* The Arbiter was a magistrate, whose especial
duty was the determination and apportionment of inherit-
ances. He is sent for by Querolus, only as a friend : but in
the concluding scene, his peculiar office is brought into play.

† The *lustrum* is the residue of the purification, in which
residue, the evil or pollution to be removed, is absorbed and
included.

dulges himself in a long soliloquy; first complaining of his master's unreasonableness in objecting to petty thefts and waste of property: in keeping strict accounts, and requiring the full change of his money: in begrudging his domestics their own quantities of sleep and wine: in requiring them, when he gives them holidays, to return to their day: in storming, if he sees finger-marks on his drinking-cups: in discovering immediately, if an amphora has been cracked and sealed up again, or if an abstracted portion of wine has been replaced by water: in detecting abrasions of silver and gold. And his friend the Arbiter is worse than himself. He gives half-allowance of food and double allowance of work. Querolus feeds his household well, and is not exacting of hard labour. He is the best of the two, but too much given to scolding, and too liberal with his whip. But the life of domestic slaves is not so bad as some think. They are thought drowsy and stupid, because they sleep in the day. But this they do, because they keep it up at night. The night is their day. Then they bathe, then they feast, then they enjoy themselves. The worst of thieves are masters, who sit up late themselves, and steal part of the night from their servants. In many respects, the master is their servant. He has to find the revenue, they have to consume it.

He then fancies he hears his master calling, to know why he loiters; and thinking it very hard that he cannot take his own time about his errand,

utters a string of maledictions, and takes his
departure.

Now come in the three rogues, and Querolus
with the box.

Mand. Lay down the burthen. Thou hast done enough
  To satisfy religion, in thyself
  Aiding to bear Ill Fortune out of doors.
Quer. Thy art is mighty. What a sudden weight
  Has come into this box ! 'Twas light for one,
  And now o'erburthens two.
Mand.   Dost thou not know
  Nothing is heavier than Evil Fortune?
Quer. Too well I know it.
Mand.   The Gods favour thee.
  No house was ever purified as thine is.
  All the bad luck it held is here made fast.
  We'll bear it to the river's deepest pool,
  Where its own weight shall send it to the bottom.
  But Evil Fortune, even from that depth,
  May rise to trouble thee. Therefore observe,
  To keep thy doors close bolted night and day,
  Till three days end. Admit nor friends nor kindred:
  Not even Good Fortune, shouldst thou hear her
    knocking.
  That period past, thy house is clear for ever.
Quer. I shall observe.
Mand.   Shut close. Bars, locks, and chains.
Quer. No fastening shall be spared. Farewell, great
  Master.

The accomplices are now in undisturbed possession of their prize. They had kept Querolus
out of the sacrarium, while they whipped the urn
into the box; and now determine on proceeding
to a solitary spot on the river-side, where they may

break up the vessel, and after abstracting the treasure, sink the fragments in some unfathomable pool.

These being gone, Pantolabus comes in with the Arbiter. In reply to some inquiries of the Arbiter concerning his master, Pantolabus thanks him for the good advice he gives, and the good example he sets, to Querolus, in relation to the treatment of servants.

Pant. Would that he had your manners: were as gracious,
Indulgent, patient, kind, as you with yours.
Arb. I take your praise, Pantolabus, at its value :
You do me too much honour.
Pant.   We all know you,
And give you all the thanks you so well merit.
Would all we have wished for you might betide you !
Arb. And may you feel, in your own bones and skins,
Whatever favours you would shower on me.

Pantolabus excuses himself from any double meaning. The Arbiter is satisfied. He expresses his surprise at finding the doors closed. They knock, and call, and receive no answer. Pantolabus conducts him to a small back-door, which, even if that be also closed, he knows how to open.

The accomplices return, full of lamentation and superstitious terror. They had dug up, and carried off, a funeral urn.

Mand. Oh me, unhappy !
Syc.   Oh me, miserable !
Sard. Oh me, most miserable, naked and shipwrecked !
Mand. Oh, Sycophanta !
Syc.   Oh, Sardanapalus !

Sard. Oh, great Mandrogerus—father and master !
Unhappy comrades, veil your heads in mourning.
This is much worse than to have lost a man.
This is the loss of losses.* Where are now
Your hopes of power and wealth? All turned to ashes.
False hope has barbed the sting of poverty.
Mand. Lay down, poor friends, your melancholy burthen.
Our tears are due to this cinereal urn.
Oh, most false treasure ! have I followed thee
Through seas and winds? Made prosperous naviga-
tion?
Magic and mathematics have I studied,
That buried men might cheat me? And expounded
Their fate to others, ignorant of my own?
Here is a buried father. I, who wept not
My own, now mourn a stranger's. Querolus
Mourns not, to whom alone this grief is due.
Sard. Oh, cruel treasure ! What was the disease
That carried thee from life? What funeral pyre
Turned thee to ashes? Us, thy expectant heirs,
Why hast thou disinherited, oh treasure?
Whether shall we, cut off without a sesterce,
Now bend our steps ?
Mand.   Look to the urn once more.
Read over the inscription.
Sard.   Funeral relics
I cannot touch : nothing I dread so deeply.
Syc. Thou hast a timid soul, Sardanapalus.

* — majore domus gemitu, majore tumultu,
Planguntur nummi, quam funera. Nemo dolorem
Fingit in hoc casu, vestem deducere summam
Contentus, vexare oculos humore coacto.
Ploratur lacrimis amissa pecunia veris.
                                   JUV. xiii. 130-134.
Feigned sorrow oft in funeral rites appears ;
The loss of gold is wept with real tears.

(*Reads*) HERE LIES TRIERINUS, SON OF TRI-
CIPITINUS,
DEPOSITED AND BURIED.   Oh me, miserable !
My heart is in my throat.   The smell of gold,
I have heard, is always sweet : * but this is redolent
Of dire aromata ; † even through the mass
Of treacherous lead,‡ that covers down the ashes.

Mand. So well perfumed, the dead has been much honoured.

Syc.   Had I but listened to the magpie's warning,
I had not fall'n in this calamity.

Sard.   Nor I, had I obeyed the admonition
Given me this morning by a crop-tailed dog.

Mand. What admonition?

Sard.   As I left the house,
He ran between my legs, and tripped me backward.

Mand. What had I done to thee, old Euclio,
Thou shouldst deride me in thy life and death ?

Syc.   What shall we do now ?

Mand.   What remains to us,
But to revenge ourselves on Euclio's son,
And make us pastime of his credulous fear ?
Peep in, and mark.   Take care he sees you not.

Sard.   He and his men are ranged within the doors,
All armed with rods and cudgels.

Mand.   Keeping guard
'Gainst Evil Fortune.   Now approach, and frighten
them.
Say thou art she, and threaten to break in.

* —————— Lucri bonus est odor ex re
            Qualibet.   JUV. xiv. 204, 5.
Alluding to the well-known anecdote of Vespasian.—
Sueton, Vesp. 23.

† Alluding to the sweet herbs which it was customary to
lay over the ashes ; and which may have been placed in the
urn by Euclio, to increase the deception.

‡ The lead was well imagined, to give probability to the
apparent weight.

Sard.   Ho ! Querolus ?
Quer.   Who calls ?
Sard.   Quick ! let me in.
Quer. For what ?
Sard.   That I may enter my old quarters.
Quer. Zeta ! Pantolabus ! stand by the doors,
Hence, Evil Fortune ! whither the Great Master
Conveyed thee.
Sard.   He predicted my return ;
And I am here.
Quer.   Wert thou Good Fortune even,
Thou shouldst not enter.
Mand.   Thunder at the door,
To draw the men aside, while through the window
We cast this funeral urn.   Oh, Querolus !
Receive the treasure which old Euclio left thee,
Such wealth be ever thine, and such thy children's.
Now, all on board, lest from this sacrilege
Arise some peril to our liberties.

They make off accordingly ; but Sardanapalus
cannot be satisfied, unless he enjoys the terror of
Querolus, on receiving through his window a visit
from the dead.   He puts his ear to the door.   He
is astounded by shouts of joy and the jingling of
gold.   The broken urn has scattered its contents
on the floor.   He hastens back to his comrades ;
thinking that if he remains, he may be apprehended
for a thief, without having the pleasure of their
company.
    The Lar enters again :—

Lar.   The urn has yielded up its weight of gold ;
Rendered true faith to its depositor ;
Deluded the deluders ; robbed the thieves,

The simulated death gives the son life,
Restoring what the living father hid.
Hence let men learn, that none may win or lose,
But by the will of a divinity.*
My office is absolved to Querolus;
But now that thief and cheat, Mandrogerus,
Will I draw thither, to put forth his claim
To half the treasure, on old Euclio's letter,
Where he shall find himself in deep dilemma,
And bear the burthen of his own misdeed.

Querolus, and his friend the Arbiter, enter, discussing the circumstances of the buried treasure, the
provident device of Euclio, the singular modes of
abstraction and restoration. Mandrogerus enters,
and after some preliminary, presents the letter.
Querolus reads it :

' Euclio bids health to his son, Querolus.
Dreading to trust a stranger, or a slave,
I send my faithful friend, Mandrogerus,
To show thee, without fraud, what I have left thee.
This being done, give him one half the treasure,
In compensation of his faith and pains.'

Quer. You were, abroad, my father's friend and comrade ?
Mand. The letter shows it.
Quer.   Show me, then, the treasure
Which we are to divide.
Mand.   I have delivered it
Untouched to you.
Quer.   Indeed !
Mand.   Do you deny it ?
Quer. To me? an untouched treasure ? Why, what treasure?
Mand. That which your father left.

* There's a divinity that shapes our ends,
  Rough-hew them how we may.

Quer. Where is it, then ?
Here is the Arbiter, to make partition.
Mand. I say 'tis in your hands.
Quer. From yours ?
Mand. From mine.
Quer. 'Twas in your hands, then ?
Mand. Yes, and might have stay'd there :
The whole : I only claim my honest share.
Quer. You stir not hence until you render it.
Mand. Why, I have rendered it.
Quer. To whom ? When ? How ?
Mand. To-day. Here. Through the window.
Quer. Whence, then, came it ?
Mand. From the sacrarium.
Quer. How went it thence ?
Mand. Out through the door. You bore it out yourself.
Quer. You were to show it to me without fraud.
But this is idle talk. The thing appears not.
Where is this treasure ?
Mand. I have given it to thee.
I swear by all the gods. 'Twas in an urn.
I pitched it through the window.
Quer. Brave confession !
This, then, is he, oh worthy Arbiter !
Who hurled into my house that funeral urn.
Pantolabus, the fragments.—Can you read
What here is written ?
Mand. I have read, and read it.

" HERE LIES TRIERINUS, SON OF TRICIPITINUS,
DEPOSITED AND BURIED."

Quer. Not content
With failing in your duty to the living,
You have made sport and mockery of the dead ;
Broken into the tomb ; dug up the ashes ;
Borne them abroad into the public way ;
Stolen the treasure which was buried with them ;

And hurled the fatal relics through the window,
To scatter on the floor, and thus pollute
The house thou first hadst plundered.
Mand.   Fare thee well.
I seek no more.   Fortune abandons me.

Querolus, however, will not let him go.   They
examine and cross-examine him ; threaten to take
him to the prætor; but give him the choice of the
charge which they shall make against him, whether
it shall be for robbery or sacrilege.   He tries a
defence on each charge severally, and gives up
both points in despair, leaving it to them to charge
him with whichever they please—either the theft,
which he could not commit, or the sacrilege, which
he would not have committed.   But he throws
himself on their mercy, and only entreats to be
allowed to depart.   The Arbiter now intercedes
for him, as having been really, however unfaith-
fully, the means of Querolus's wealth.   And
Querolus, who had been previously disposed to be
generous towards him, agrees to give him main-
tenance, and receive him into his household.

Sycophanta and Sardanapalus then present themselves.   They solicit a small participation in
Querolus's bounty.   They are aware, that one
house does not take three hungry idlers ; but they
implore a moderate donation, to speed them on
another quest.   Querolus replies :

Let the beaten parasite
Have compensation for his injuries.

And immediately follows a sort of epilogue, in the form of a senatus-consultum, fixing a tariff of compensation for torn clothes, bruises, broken bones, and all other forms of injury to which parasites are liable. This was most probably subjoined as an exposition of Querolus's last words.

In this view of the conclusion, we follow the old reading : *Mercedem vulnerum victus recipiat Parasitus. In convivio si fuerit veste discissus,* &c. Klinkhämer terminates the comedy thus :

——— vulnerum mercedem victus recipiat.

Pauca desiderantur.

And after some preliminary, presents the final passage as a *pannus assutus :*

PARASITUS.   In convivio si fuerit, &c.

Three of the editors of this comedy, and many other writers, have spoken of it in the highest terms of praise. Gruter and Pareus disparaged it. Cannegetier thinks that "none can disparage it but those who do not understand it." The ill-humour of Gruter and Pareus appears to have been excited chiefly from the MSS. bearing on the title *Plauti Querolus ;* but this was not the fault of the author, who speaks of himself as treading in Plautus's steps. The assignment of the authorship to Plautus must have been very ancient, for Servius, in his *Commentary on Virgil* (Æn. lii. 226), cites it as *Plauti Querolus.*

Danielis calls it "a comedy, not less remarkable as a singular relic of antiquity, than admirable from the novelty of its argument." Rittershusius says, this comedy "requires no eulogium from him, being sufficiently recommended by its wonderful variety of argument, the gravity of its sentences, and the elegance of its comic diction." Klinkhämer concurs in these estimates, and adds the commendation of exemplary propriety and modesty. He expresses his surprise, that a work so well worthy to be generally read should have been left to lurk in the libraries of the curious.

Barthius panegyrizes "the simple elegance and acute sense of the colloquies, and their excellent adaptation to the several characters of the speakers — adding, that "the more it is read, the more its sense and eloquence will be perceived."

Klinkhämer's pains on this comedy have been worthily and successfully bestowed. We feel grateful to him, for the form in which he has presented it to us; and shall be highly gratified if our readers shall derive, from our necessarily limited exposition, any portion of the pleasure which we have received from the work itself.

G

No. II.

[Published in *Fraser's Magazine* for April 1852.]

THE PHAETHON OF EURIPIDES.

IT had long been known that there existed in
the library at Paris a manuscript called the *Codex
Claromontanus*, containing an inedited fragment,
or fragments, of Euripides; and many reclama-
tions on the subject had been uttered from Germany, but without any result, till Immanuel Bekker,
passing through Paris, transcribed it, and commu-
nicated it to Hermann, who subsequently received
from H. Hasius a copy representing the MS. according to the exact trace of the letters.   Fortified
with this indispensable basis of correction, Hermann revised and edited the contents of the MS.
with his own emendations in 1821; and thus
brought the world acquainted with two large fragments of the Phaëthon.*   Immediately on their

---

* Twelve years ago, we received the following note from a
classical friend, who was not at the time aware of Hermann's
publication :—

"—— What is the *Merops* of Eripides about?   Of
the Greek MSS. in the King's Library at Paris—which anybody may examine for asking—No. 107 contains St Paul's
Epistles, and two leaves at least, ff. 162-3, are obviously
Palimpsest.   The two leaves consist of four pages, and each
page of two columns of the original writing, which is in large
letters, and comprises a portion of the *Merops* of Euripides.
At the rate of only twenty-five lines in a column, there are
two hundred verses : what a noble fragment !

i

publication, he transmitted a copy to Goethe, who, being struck by their extraordinary beauty, arranged them, and the previously known fragments of the same tragedy, according to his own view of their proper order; translated them into verse, filling up a few of the *lacunæ* with additions of his own; and connected the series by an analytical exposition of the probable progress of the drama.

"The second writing is of the fifth century. If we allow the first writing to be only a little more than half as old again, it may be the autograph of the Tragedian himself. But you will know the poet's hand, when you see it !

"This information was given about a century ago by Montfaucon, who adds, that in the margin may plainly be seen several times, Merops, Chorus, and θεραπων — the names of the interlocutors. This he relates as a matter of mere curiosity, not having any idea how easily erased writing may be restored and read. So his examination was cursory (there was no motive then to make any other), and a careful search will probably discover many more than two rescribed leaves.

"The information of Montfaucon has not been noticed, I believe, by any person, except one Bruns, a learned German, who cried out lustily about it some fifty years ago, from a remote corner of Germany, to Villoison. If V. had heard him, he would most likely have had a touch at the MS.

"The printed catalogue of the French King's MSS. does not remark that this is palimpsest, nor is it usual; but it states that several leaves were stolen formerly, and sold to the owner of the Harleian Collection, and on learning of the theft, the Earl of Oxford liberally returned them. This anecdote is very remarkable, and if any portion of the lost Tragedy was abstracted, only not miraculous."

[This letter must be from the pen of Thomas Jefferson Hogg.—G.]

Since that period there have been several editions of the fragments of Euripides, in which the remains of this tragedy have been arranged according to the views of the respective editors. The same task is performed in the valuable and elaborate work of Hartung, *Euripides Restitutus.* The latest edition of the fragments of Euripides is that of Wagner. We shall give our own view of the fragments of *Phaëthon,* noticing incidentally any essential points of difference in the arrangement,

The prologue was most probably spoken by Oceanus, the father of Clymene. Phaëthon, to whom Hartung assigns it, could not have spoken it, because he could not know all the previous circumstances of his history. This perfect knowledge of the past is indispensable to the speaker of the prologue ; and in cases where no mortal can possess it, Euripides assigns the task to a spirit or a deity—as to the ghost of Polydorus to reveal the history of his murder, or to Venus to solve the mystery of Phaedra's affliction. Clymene, to whom Ravius and others assign it, might have spoken the prologue ; but as the only fragment cited from it presents her in the accusative case, this supposition becomes at least doubtful, although the passage may admit the personal pronoun. " Euripides," says Strabo, "represents Clymene to have been given in marriage to Merops." Clymene might have spoken of herself as having been so given, though Strabo, in introducing the passage, would necessarily substitute "Clymene" for "me." Goethe, who, on the basis of the few lines remaining, has constructed a long and mainly original prologue, assigns it to the warder, watching and announcing the dawn, and reciting circumstances publicly and generally known. This, however, is losing sight of the true character of the Euripidean prologue, in all cases where the subsequent action has its basis in the revelation of a fatal secret.

The prologue, then, may have been spoken by Clymene: but most probably it was spoken by Oceanus, and recited the love of the Sun-god for Clymene; the promise which she exacted from him, that he would grant one request to one child of their union; the birth of their four children, three daughters, Lampetia, Aegle, and Phaëthusa, and one son, Phaëthon; that Clymene had been given in marriage to Merops sufficiently long before the birth of Phaëthon to make him think the child his own; that Merops was then occupied in preparations for Phaëthon's marriage with a young goddess, which was to take place that day; that Phaëthon was determined not to marry above his rank, but to seek his fortune in other lands; that Clymene, terrified by this resolve of her son, would reveal to him the secret of his birth, out of which would arise perils to Clymene requiring the presence of her father, Oceanus, to watch over and avert.

The first of the old fragments belongs to this prologue :—

―――― Clymene was given in marriage
To Merops, monarch of this ocean-shore :
The land which first, from his four-steeded car,
The ascending Sun strikes with his golden fire.
This land the neighbouring black-complexioned men
Call the Sun's Stables and the Realm of Morning.

The kingdom of Merops was, therefore, conterminal to the dominions of the Sun. That this vicinity was innocuous is expressed in another fragment, which also apparently belongs to the prologue :—

The Sun's fierce flame, ascending o'er the earth,
Most burns the distant lands : with gentler ray
Tempering the near.

The prologue is followed by a dialogue between Clymene and her son, in which Phaëthon urges his objections to the proposed marriage, chiefly, it would seem, on account of his inferiority in birth to his bride, who is evidently a goddess, and most probably Aurora. This may be inferred from verse 135. We have numbered the verses for convenience of reference. The following three fragments appear to belong to this scene, and to have been spoken by Phaëthon :—

Phaëthon. The free-born man becomes a slave by marriage,
Sold for a dowry to a loftier name.
A heavy doom is stamped upon the rich,
To lose the clearness of their mental sight.
Is it that Fortune, being blind herself,
Gives her own blindness where she showers her
favours ?

The air is everywhere the eagle's path *
And every land is to the brave his country.

* This first line is added, and the second modified, from the fragments of uncertain dramas.

We now come to the first of the two great fragments from the *Codex Claromontanus.* The same
scene continues :—

Clymene.	I give this counsel,

Remembering the promise which he made me.
Ask then, one favour—whatsoe'er thou wilt :
One only : more thou must not seek to gain.
If this be granted, thou wilt truly know
Thy Father is the Sun ; if not, thy mother
Has spoken falsely.

Phaëthon. How shall I approach
The burning dwelling of the god of day ?

Clymene. 'Twill be his care to keep thee safe from harm.

Phaëthon. Thou say'st well, if he be indeed my sire.

Clymene. The truth will be in time made plain to thee.

Phaëthon. Enough. I am satisfied thou speak'st not lightly.
Return into the palace ; for the handmaids
Are coming forth, who, while the monarch slum-
bers,
Sweep down his dwelling, and with daily care,
Make bright the floors and purify the walls,
And with the native odours of our land
Make all the entrance fragrant. When my father
Shall rise from sleep, and, passing through the
gates,
Shall speak to me of marriage, then, departing,
I will approach the palace of the Sun,
And learn, oh mother ! if thy words are true.

This dialogue is followed by the entrance of the
Chorus, the handmaids already mentioned, who, in
the first lyrical song, present a beautiful picture of
the life of the early morning, and celebrate the
approaching nuptials of Phaëthon.

CHORUS.

The dawn scarce glitters o'er the hills :
The nightingale, where trees embower,
Still sits in thickest shade, and fills
The air with song of gentlest power,
Pouring the soft, sad, tuneful strain,
For Itys, Itys, mourned in vain.
The reed makes music from the rocks,
As shepherds upland drive their flocks.

The colts in pairs to pasture go :
The dogs before the hunter bound :
And where the Ocean-fountains flow,*
The swan's mellifluous notes resound.
Vessels are moving on the deep :
Some by the oar's impetuous sweep ;
While some, before the favouring gale,
Stay the tall mast, and spread the sail.

.   .   .   .
.   .   .   .
.   .   .   .
.   .   .   .†

These several tasks while others ply,
'Tis mine the palace to adorn,
And sing the high solemnity,
That opens with this opening morn :
The nuptials of our sovereign's son :
The fondly-cherished, only one :
Reverence and love my voice employ,
To raise the song of festal joy.

For servants share the master's weal,
And well with song his bliss may greet :

---

* The Ocean was a great river, surrounding the earth ; and the seas were inlets from it. Being a river, it had, of course, its fountains, which are here placed on the extreme eastern shore.

† A portion of the MS. is here illegible.

Not less ordained his pains to feel,
When on him Fortune's tempests beat.
Long have I prayed this hour to see,
When masters so beloved by me
Might see the torch of Hymen glow :
Time brings about, and gods bestow
On my lord's son the nuptial bond :
Let song to song in joy respond.

Silence awhile : for from the palace gates,
Preceded by the sacred Herald, come
The monarch and his son. The king will speak
His sense of what befits the auspicious day,
When Phaëthon receives his heaven-born bride.

Merops and Phaëthon now come from the palace, preceded by the herald, who calls on the people to assemble, and listen in silence to the voice of the king.

Herald. People, by Jove's bounty placed
On this Ocean-bordering plain,
Hither from your dwellings haste :
Reverence this benignant reign.
I the nuptial rite declare—
Happy issue thence I pray—
Which the father and his heir
Come to celebrate to-day.
All around in silence stand :
Hear the monarch of the land.

Of the oration of Merops only four words are legible in the *Codex :*—

If I speak well.

But two of the previously known fragments may be most probably assigned to this oration of Merops.

> I count not him among the wise of mortals,
> Who, as a father to ill-minded children,
> Or, as a king, to subjects, gives free licence.
> One anchor does not hold a ship as safely
> As that which lays out three.*   A single chief
> Is to a city a precarious guard :
> A second, equal-minded, serves it well.

From which it would seem that Merops informed the people of his intention not only to unite his son to a bride of exalted birth, but to give him an equal share of his throne.

Goethe assigns these passages, and several others, to a dialogue between the Sun and Phaëthon, supposing the scene changed for a time to the Solar Palace. The political reflections thus put

---

* Pindar says (*Ol.* vi.)—"Two anchors are good to hold by in stormy weather." Boeckh expounds : "One from the head, and one from the stern." This would lay the ship broadside on to the sea, and swamp her. He must have been thinking of a ship moored head and stern in a tide-river. This mistake has been copied by subsequent editors ; showing that knowledge of words alone will not suffice for an expositor, without some knowledge of the subject-matter. It would be curious to see how Boeckh and his followers would deal with Euripides's third anchor : whether they would lay it out from amidships. We remember a facetious publication, in which a lady asks her learned husband, "whether the Greeks saw sun, moon, and stars, sea, rivers, fields, and trees, as we do?" "Yes, my dear," he replies, "they saw the same things as we do, but they saw them in Greek." "Bless me!" says the lady, "that must have been very puzzling." It is only through this sort of Greek medium that our learned professors could have seen a ship riding out a gale of wind.

into the mouth of the Sun he thinks very much
out of place—which makes it the more singular
that he should so have assigned them. The
change of scene, also, from the Palace to Merops
of that of the Sun, and back to the Palace of
Merops, is contrary to the principles of the Greek
drama, is altogether unnecessary, and destroys the
simplicity of the tragedy.

With respect to the scene between Merops and
Phaëthon, Goethe observes: "Unfortunately the
next scene is all but lost: but it is easy to see
that its dramatic capabilities were great. A father
who has prepared for his son a magnificent
marriage-festival, and a son who has declared to
his mother that in the midst of these preparations it is his intention to steal away and under-
take a perilous adventure, present the most
intensely-striking opposing influences, of which it
can scarcely be doubted Euripides took full advantage in the development of the dialogue."

Goethe proceeds to assign to this dialogue the
arguments of Phaëthon against marriage, which,
concurring with Wagner and Bothe, we have
assigned to the preceding scene with Clymene.
It is not probable that Phaëthon stated his objections to the proposed marriage to Merops: his
purpose was, apparently, to accomplish it, if he
should find himself equal in birth to his goddess-
bride: he would therefore have dissembled with
his supposed father, reserving to himself the ulti-
mate decision on the result of his interview with

the Sun, which he might safely do, as the completion of the ceremony was reserved for the evening. Merops, indeed, as is evident from subsequent fragments, went on uninterruptedly and unsuspiciously with the preparations for the marriage.

Phaëthon has departed : has obtained from his reluctant father permission to drive the chariot of the Sun : and early in his ascent has been struck down by a thunderbolt from Jupiter. There is now a long break in the series of fragments : but one of the fragments of uncertain dramas appears to belong to this part of the tragedy.

> The form, late flourishing in youthful beauty,
> Has like a falling-star been quenched, and poured
> Its living breath on the ethereal waste.

We may assume that a thunder-peal has been heard, and that something has been seen in the distance. " Hurled headlong flaming from the ethereal sky." Clymene and the chorus understand the catastrophe : but it is probable that a messenger announces the particulars. Another uncertain fragment may perhaps be placed here.

> Many has thunder's bloodless wound destroyed.

The fragment next in order belongs to Clymene.

> The corpse of him most dear to me is left,
> To rot, unwashed, amid accessless rocks.

This passage is preserved by Plutarch, who quotes it as not agreeing with the received opinion, that bodies killed by thunder do not decay, and that neither beasts nor birds will touch them.

In another fragment Clymene abhors the sight of everything which reminds her of her son.

> I hate the well-slung bow of corneil-wood :
> All sports, all games, are horrid to my thoughts.

The presence of the bow reminded her of the exercises in which Phaëthon had acquired the daring which led to his destruction.

We now come to the second of the great fragments of the *Codex Claromontanus.*

The body of Phaëthon is brought in, and continues to exhale a sulphureous smoke.

The sight redoubles the grief of Clymene, and at the same time fills her with terror for herself, lest the truth should become known to Merops.

Clymene. The Fatal Fury, living in the dead,
 Breathes forth the vapour of sulphureous fire.
 Oh ! I am lost. Why haste you not to bear
 The corpse within? Haste ! for my husband comes,
 Leading the virgins of the nuptial train.
 Quickly draw near, and wipe away the spots,
 If blood, perchance, have fallen on the ground.
 Oh, hasten, hasten, handmaids : I will hide him
 Within the marble chambers, where the king
 Preserves his treasure : I alone possess
 The keys. Oh, light-bestowing deity !
 How hast thou ruined me, and this, thy child !
 Well among mortals art thou called Apollo,
 By those who read the mystic names of gods.

The name Apollo is here alluded to as signifying Destroyer.   Cassandra makes a similar allusion in the *Agamemnon* of Æschylus.   It is to be observed, however, that the Sun and Apollo are always distinct deities in Homer and Æschylus, though Euripides, in this passage, appears to treat them as one.   We say appears, for it is not quite clear that he does so.   The last line, more literally translated, is :

> By those who know the unspoken names of gods.

And Apollo might have been the epithet of the two deities, though given openly to Phœbus, and tacitly to Helios.

The body is borne into the palace.   Clymene follows it.   Merops enters at the head of the Hymeneal Chorus.

CHORUS.

> Hymen, oh Hymen ! now we sing,
> Thee, of the bridal train the king,
> From whom all bliss proceeds ;
> And her, Jove's daughter, heavenly bright,
> Venus, who to the nuptial rite
> The happy virgin leads.
> Oh, Cypria, ever young and fair,
> O loveliest of the queens of heaven !
> To thee I raise the choral prayer ;
> And to thy son, to whom is given,
> In links of mutual love to bind
> The sons and daughters of mankind.
> Oh Hymen, Venus, Love ! combine
> To bless our ancient sovereign's line,
> And honour, in this regal dome,
> The bride who leaves her starry home,

Our youthful lord to grace.
Greater is his than monarch's pride,
Who gains the love of such a bride:
Alone of earthly race,
Who weds a daughter of the sky:
Whom mortals and immortals vie
To bless: whose peerless high estate
Earth's utmost bounds shall celebrate.

Merops. Go thou: lead in these damsels: bid the queen
With solemn Hymeneal dance and song
Surround the altars of the gods, within
The palace, and the sacred seat of Vesta
First, as the truly pious always use,
Approach with prayer . . .
   .   .   .   .   .   .*
   .   . from my house be given,
A dower worthy the celestial bride.

Attendant. Oh king! in haste my steps have left the palace:
For, from the marble chambers of the treasure
Pour, through the joints and fissures of the doors,
Thick streaks of blackening smoke: showing
   within
No trace of flame: but fume of smouldering ashes.
But hasten inwards, lest the sudden wrath
Of Vulcan should involve the walls in fire,
Amidst these happy nuptials of thy son.

Merops. How say you? See that you have not mistaken
The smoke of sacrifice, which I have ordered
From all the altars, for this smoke you speak of.

Attendant. I have well noted. All is clear, except
As I have said.

Merops. Knows my wife this, or not?

Attendant. The queen is all intent on sacrifice.

Merops. I go, then: such beginnings, if neglected,
May lead to fearful ends. Oh, Queen of Fire!

---

* MS. illegible.

Daughter of Ceres ! and thou, bounteous Vulcan !
Look on my dwelling with benignant eyes.

Merops goes in, and the Chorus expresses its
fears. The Chorus of Virgins, which sung the
Hymeneal Song, appears to have gone back into
the palace, and the Chorus of Female Slaves in the
confidence of Clymene, who had assisted her to
carry in the body, and had left the stage to the
Hymeneal Chorus, have now returned to their
place.

CHORUS.

Oh misery ! oh misery !
Where shall I stay my flying feet ?
How, where no mortal eye their trace can see,
In air, or earth's profound obscurity,
    Find an inscrutable retreat ?
Alas ! alas ! the wretched queen,
And her dead son, in vain concealed,
Her grief, her shame will now be seen,
And all the fearful truth revealed.
Revealed will be the Sun's illicit love,
The fire-imprinted wound, the lightning-brand of Jove.
Oh wretched with immeasurable grief,
Daughter of Ocean ! to thy Father spread
Thy hands in prayer, to speed to thy relief,
And chase the perils which o'erhang thy head.
Merops (*within*).   Alas ! alas !

CHORUS.

        Hear'st thou the monarch's groans ?
Merops. My child !

CHORUS.

He calls on him who cannot hear :
Who lies before him, manifest in death.

Here ends the Claromontane manuscript. A few previously known fragments remain. One belongs to Merops :

> The acclaiming multitude drove from my mind
> My own subjection to calamity.*

The rest belong most probably to the final speech of Oceanus, who intervenes to reconcile Merops to Clymene, and explain the circumstances of Phaëthon's fate. It is clear that what passed between the son and father, during the ascent of the chariot of the Sun, could be known only to a deity. We therefore think Wagner and Hartung are in error in assigning these passages to the mortal messenger who announced to Clymene the fall of Phaëthon. Herein we concur with Bothe ; but we cannot concur with him in thinking that the tragedy was closed by an epilogue from the Sun. There is neither ground nor precedent for the intervention of two deities.†

Oceanus then narrates the Sun's reception of Phaëthon, and Phaëthon's exaction of the promise

---

* Southey expresses a similar sentiment in the "Curse of Kehama : "

> For nature in his pride has dealt the blow,
> And taught the Master of Mankind to know,
> Even he himself is man, and not exempt from woe.

† The Hippolytus is not in point, two deities both favourable to the same persons. Venus opens it as an avenger, and Diana closes it as a comforter. Each has her own distinct interest in the case ; but Oceanus and the Sun had an equal interest in Clymene.

made to his mother. The Sun had urged him to
desist from his rash purpose.

> Touch not the reins, my child, unskilled to hold them,
> Nor mount the car thou hast not learned to guide.

The next passage is preserved by Longinus :
" The Sun, giving the reins to Phaëthon, says :—

> " Drive not within the Lybian atmosphere ;
> Having no moisture, 'twill not bear thy wheels,
> But send them downward. *

" And further on :—

> " Direct thy course on the seven Pleiades.
> This having heard, he seized the reins, and struck
> The fire-winged steeds, and launched them on their
>   course,
> Along the folds of their ethereal way.
> The sire, behind, rode by the Sirian † star,

* This seems to imply, that the elastic force of the vapour,
generated in a moist atmosphere by the heat of the solar car,
tended to give it buoyancy. There is another passage, *Inc.
Fab. Frag.* 46, in which the breath of water and fire is
enumerated among the things that are mighty :—

   Δειναὶ δὲ ποταμοῦ καὶ πυρὸς ϑερμοῦ πνοαί :

which Wagner thinks remarkable, as tending to show that
the power of steam was known to the Athenians.

† Sirius, immediately before his cosmical rising, was, poetically considered, close behind the Sun. The Sun, therefore,
riding either with or before Sirius, was in the best position
to advise his son to whom he had abandoned the absolute
guidance of the car.—See the postscript to this article.

Used singly, and without any explanatory adjunct, ὁ ἀστήρ
signifies the sun, and το ἄστρον the dog star ; but the adjective ἀστρικύς is simply starry, and belongs to no star in
particular.

Admonishing his son : ' Tend thitherward ;
This way direct the chariot ; this way, now.'

" Would you not say that the spirit of the poet ascends the chariot with Phaëthon, and sharing his peril flies with the fire-winged steeds? for unless it were carried in equal course with these celestial works it could not present such vivid phantasies."

To this narration we may assign a remarkable fragment, cited by Athenæus without the name of the play, being part of a description of the horses of the Sun.

One of flower-loving Bacchus,
. Æthops, who ripens the autumnal grapes,
Whose name men give to wine. *

It would seem, that one of the four horses was separately dominant in each of the four seasons, and that each had its own tutelar deity.

The last preserved passage must be very near the close of the speech of Oceanus, and relates to the burial of Phaëthon under the shade of his sisters, metamorphosed into poplars.

Cool-shadowing trees
Shall spread their fond arms o'er his loved remains.

That this portion of the fable was adopted both by Æschylus and Euripides, we have the authority of Pliny.

Æschylus had preceded Euripides in the treatment of this subject, in the tragedy of the *Heliades : the Daughters of the Sun.*

* See the frequent αἴθοπα οἶνον in Homer.

Of this tragedy too little is preserved to enable us to form an idea of its plan.

The three sisters of Phaëthon might have formed the Chorus, as the three Furies form that of the *Eumenides.* We do not agree with those learned Germans, who are for resolving every Chorus into one Procrustean number. We think the Chorus of the *Eumenides* was three, and that of the Suppliants fifty. Of this hereafter. Hermann thinks the sisters of Phaëthon could not have formed the Chorus, because the Chorus must remain to the end, and the metamorphosis of the sisters is (as above noticed) included in the tragedy. But the metamorphosis might have been the subject of prophecy, or might have commenced as the drama closed, like the sinking of the rock in Prometheus.

Æschylus makes the Po run westward into the ocean ; therefore the Ocean-nymphs might have formed the Chorus, or the Nymphs of the Po. But on the precedents of the Eumenides, the Choëphoroe, and the Suppliants, we think it most probable that the Chorus gave its title to the tragedy.

The Chorus might, however, have been more numerous, as mythologists are not agreed about the number of the sisters of Phaëthon. Hyginus makes them seven.

The Scholiast on Homer, *Od.* xvii. 208, makes Phaëthon and his three sisters the offspring of the Sun and of Rhoda, daughter of Asopus ; represents

the wandering of the solar car, the conflagration of
the earth, the striking of Phaëthon by the thunderbolt, his fall into the Po, and the incessant weeping
of his sisters, whom Jupiter, in compassion, changes
into poplars, and their tears into amber. " This
story," says the Scholiast, " is to be found in the
tragic poets ;" from which Welcker infers that, as
it is not the story of Euripides, it must have been
the story of Æschylus. But Hermann holds, that
the words of the Scholiast mean no more than that
the subject of Phaëthon had been treated by the
tragic writers, though the Scholiast gave the commonly received story in his own way.

According to Pliny, Æschylus places the Po in
Iberia, and represents it as identical with the
Rhône, and running westward into the ocean. At
the same time, it is clear from one small fragment,

> The Adrianian women shall preserve
> The form of lamentation,

that Æschylus placed the course of the Po not
far from the Adriatic. It is probable, therefore,
seeing how little at that time the Athenians knew
of Italy, that he gave the general name of Iberia to
the whole tract of country lying between the
Adriatic and the ocean-coast from the Rhône to
the Pillars of Hercules.

The most important fragment of the *Heliades* is
preserved by Athenæus, xi. p. 469, where he is
treating of the golden cup, in which the Sun passes
in slumber from west to east, under the shadow of

night, below the visible boundary of the ocean.
He gives on this subject passages of Stesi-chorus,
Antimachus, Mimnermus, Theolytus, Pherecydes,
and, amongst them, the following of Æschylus,
being unquestionably part of an address by the
Chorus to Phaëthon : we adopt Hermann's
reading :—

> Where, on the limits of the western deep,
> The golden vessel, framed by Vulcan's art,
> Awaits thy sire's descent.   When he has found
> Refuge and rest beneath the thickest gloom
> Of sacred sable-steeded Night, therein
> He holds his billowy, long, circumfluous way.

There are two fragments of uncertain dramas
which Hermann thinks may be assigned to the
Heliades : one which may be aptly addressed to
discourage the rashness of Phaëthon :—

> 'Tis wrong to bear a too swift-footed course,
> For none who fail have credit for good counsel.

The other may have been spoken by the
Heliades, comparing their fate with that of the
Pleiades, and justifying, by example, their incessant
lamentation :—

> The seven illustrious daughters
> Of Atlas wept their father's heavy toil,
> Bearing the weight of heaven ; where now they wear
> The forms of mighty splendour, wingless Pleiads.

Whatever was the plan of Æschylus, it was in
all probability confined to the fate of Phaëthon
and his sisters.   Euripides, we may agree with

Hartung, "varied and extended the argument by introducing the nuptial preparations and the peril of Clymene. Clymene became thereby the principal character. This change was the source of the many excellences by which this drama was distinguished; and how great these were, any one capable of judgment must understand from its remains."

Goethe prefaces his restoration by expressing his sense of the profound reverence with which such precious remains are to be approached, and remarking on the simple tragic grandeur of the fable, in which the action is confined to the locality, and not extended to the whole universe, as in Ovid and Nonnus, so that the interest is concentrated on the persons of the drama.

According to the view which we have taken of the arrangement, the action begins with the dawn. The discussions of Phaëthon with Clymene and Merops, and his departure for the Palace of the Sun, take place before sunrise. His fall occurs while he is yet on the ascent. The thunder-clap, and the fall, as of a meteoric mass, announce the catastrophe to Clymene and the Chorus. The early bolt of Jupiter prevents the calamities which the longer course of Phaëthon, in the later poets, inflicts on the world. The Sun apparently, however grieving for his child, resumes the vacant place, and the solar chariot continues its way through the heavens. The nuptial preparations, begun by the old king in his morning hope, are continued by him, in ignorance of the fate of his supposed son, till nearly the evening. The anguish and fears of Clymene are separated by the nuptial Chorus from the discovery of the catastrophe by Merops, his consequent mourning and anger. The intervening deity then reconciles the husband to the wife, and points to both a melancholy consolation in the eternal rest of Phaëthon under the shade of his sisters, weeping amber on his tomb.

"May after-time," says Goethe, "discover more of this inestimable work! I almost envy the happiness of those who may live to see it, and may be thereby further excited to persevere in the study of antiquity, whence solely pure education, and the advancement of the nobler humanities, are to be hoped and expected."

In this vow and in these hopes we most fully and cordially concur; thinking, as we do with Harris, that the "golden period" of Grecian greatness, within which the Athenian tragic theatre flourished, was "a providential event in honour of human nature, to show to what perfection the species might ascend." *

POSTSCRIPT.

We said we should notice, incidentally, any essential differences in the arrangement. We did not add, in the interpretation; for this would lead us too far from our present purpose into criticism

* *Hermes*, book iii. chap. v.

on various readings. This passage, however, having been the subject of much controversy, and, what is worse, of an "emendation," which has found favour, though it appears to us one of the most monstrous ever made, we hope to be excused if we make it an exception to our rule of critical abstinence.

The passage, as it stands in all the best editions of Longinus, is :

Πατὴρ δ' ὄπισθε νῶτα Σειρίου βεβὼς
"Ιππευε, παῖδα νουθετῶν.

Rutgersius (*Variæ Lectiones,* L. Bat. 1618), proposed as an emendation Σειραίου. This has been rejected by the editors of Longinus: Faber, Tollius, Pearce, More, Toup, Weiske ; and almost as unanimously adopted by the editors of the fragments : Barnes, Musgrave, Dindorf, Bothe, Wagner. It seems to us difficult to imagine a more outrageous absurdity.

Σειραῖος, or σειραφόρος ἵππος, is the outer horse on either side. The inner horse is the yoke horse. The σειραῖος occurs in Sophocles, with the addition of δέξιος, to show that it was the outer horse on the right side. Æschylus and Euripides use σειραφόρος in a general sense, as characterising either co-operation or freedom of action ; but, in a particular sense, neither of these words would be properly used without expressing the right or left side.

The Sun rode behind. Behind, with reference

to the chariot, obviously. But how can the adverb ὅπισθε be construed with νῶτα, so as to make it signify behind the back of the horse? And then what becomes of ἵππευε? How could the Sun ride behind the back of the horse, unless he rode on his tail? But if he rode on him at all, he would be a postilion to his own chariot, and take on himself a share in its guidance, which he had indisputably abandoned, wholly and exclusively, to Phaëthon.

And if he placed himself behind the horse, without riding on him at all, he would only be self-supported : floating *in vacuo*. Mythology gives all the gods vehicles : excepting only those who have wings. Apollo and Vulcan fall from heaven. Mercury never starts on his errand till he has tied on his *talaria*.

We concur with the editors of Longinus in rejecting Rutgersius's emendations and in adhering to the MS. reading, Σειρίου.

We concur with Toup and Weiske in rejecting the interpretation which some have given to Σείριος, *equus astricus*. If this had been otherwise correct, Euripides would not have used the term vaguely : he would have specified the star to which the horse belonged. But there is no authority for such an interpretation ; nor for supposing that the Sun had any rest-horses, like a modern four-in-hand. His four steeds were immortal and unchangeable, like himself.

The literal translation of the passage, as it stands in Longinus, is :

> The Father, behind, having gone on the back of Sirius,
> Rode, advising his son.

It is difficult to imagine the God of Day riding on the back of a dog : even of the *Canis Cælestis*.

But the name Sirius does not necessarily suggest the idea of a dog. If Σείριος be correctly derived from Σείρ "Sol, teste Suida" (Steph. *Thes.* ed. Valpy. p. 8288), Σείριος ἀστήρ is *Stella Solaris*, the Star peculiarly belonging to the Sun, as his auxiliary in the diffusion of heat. " This Star is also called the Dog of Orion : " but Sirius is another name of the Star, not the name of the Dog.

In passages where poetical dignity is given to the personified Star, he is called only Sirius. Quintus Smyrnaeus seems to give a chariot and horses to Sirius in the passage cited by Toup :

> Οἷος δ'ἐκ περάτων ἀναφαίνεται Ὠκεανοῖο
> Ἥλιος, θηητῶν ἐπὶ χθόνα πῦρ ἀμαρύσσων,
> Πῦρ, ὅτε οἱ πώλοισι καὶ ἅρμασι συμφέρετ' ἀστήρ
> Σείριος————.

" As the Sun appears, rising up from the limits of ocean, radiating splendid fire on the earth : when the Star Sirius is borne, together with him, by horses and chariots,"—*i.e.*, when the chariots and horses of Sirius and the Sun run side by side along the circle of the sky.

The MSS. of Longinus have all ὄπισθεν ὦτα, from which the editors have made ὄπισθε νῶτα, dropping the aspirate.

A reading, still nearer to the MSS. than that which has been adopted, would be ὄπισθ᾽ ἐν ᾧ τὰ :

Πατὴρ δ᾽ ὄπισθ᾽ ἐν ᾧ τὰ Σειρίου βεβὼς
"Ιππευε, παῖδα νουθετῶν.

" The Father, having gone behind, in that part of the sky in which were the *res Sirii* (Sirius himself, his chariot and horses), rode, admonishing his son." We suggest this, with all deference : but we think it a presentable lection.

The Greeks computed their canicular days from the heliacal rising of Sirius—the time when his rising first becomes visible in the morning twilight —which is not till he is about fifteen degrees in advance of the Sun : in other words, when the Sun is about fifteen degrees below the horizon, at the time of the rising of the Star.

The cosmical rising of Sirius (the time when he rises with the Sun) is therefore about fifteen days earlier than the heliacal. Intermediately, the Star, being in the path of the Sun, is lost in the splendour of his rays.

At Athens, in the time of Euripides, the heliacal rising of Sirius, by an approximate computation, occurred in the beginning of July : the cosmical, consequently, just after the middle of June.

It occurred, therefore, before the close of the period within which the nightingale sings : the season distinctly marked in the beginning of the tragedy, vv. 41-45.

Immediately before his cosmical rising, Sirius, as we have said, poetically considered, was close behind the Solar chariot.

Ἱππεύειν is used for riding in a chariot. Ἥλιος ἀνιππεύων, in the prologue of Ion, is the rising Sun.

If we were to make a picture in our minds of the position, we should place the chariot of Sirius behind the chariot of the Sun, a little on one side: the horses of Sirius abreast of the solar wheels: Sirius, not as a dog, but as a sidereal deity; and Helios standing by him in the chariot, on the side nearest to Phaëthon.

No. III.

[Published in *Fraser's Magazine* for October 1857.]

THE "FLASK" OF CRATINUS.

Prisco si credis, Mæcenas docte, Cratino,
Nulla placere diu, nec vivere carmina possunt,
Quæ scribuntur aquæ potoribus : ut male sanos
Adscripsit Liber Satyris Faunisque poetas.
Vina fere dulces oluerunt mane Camœnæ.
Laudibus arguitur vini vinosus Homerus.
Ennius ipse pater nunquam, nisi potus, ad arma
Prosiluit dicenda.   Forum puteaIque Libonis
Mandabo siccis, adimam cantare severis.

No water-drinker's verse, if faith you give
To old Cratinus, long can please, or live.
Bacchus assigned to bards, at most half-sane,
Their place with Fauns and Satyrs in his train.
Homer so praises wine, you clearly tell
By that alone, he liked it passing well.

Old Ennius ne'er sprang forth of arms to sing,
Without the aid that strong potations bring.
Let those who drink not, and austerely dine,
Dry up in law : the Muses smell of wine.
Hor. Epist. I. 19.

CUMBERLAND translates Πυτίνη flagon : but, as it
had a wicker coat, it was more properly a flask ;
much larger, however, than anything we are accus-
tomed to call so.   It was, in fact, a flask in con-
struction, and a flagon in capacity; a sort of
pocket-pistol for Pantagruel.

The loss of this comedy is one of the greatest in
the wreck of the Greek drama ; not merely from
what must have been its intrinsic value, but from the
remarkable circumstances attending its production.

Aristophanes, in a parabasis of the *Knights*, re-
proached the Athenians with their neglect of their
most illustrious comic poets when they had grown
old and past the power of dramatic production ;
and instanced Cratinus, who had once, amidst
their tumultuous applause, rushed along in an
irresistible torrent, uprooting oaks, and planes, and
enemies ; when, in all festivals, nothing was heard
but some of his choral songs ; and now that his
intellect was dimmed, and his lyre was unstrung,
and his coronal was dry, and himself as dry as his
coronal, perishing with thirst, they had no pity for
him ; whereas, for the sake of his former victories,
he ought to be drinking in the Prytaneum, and
seated in becoming apparel in the most honourable
place of the theatre.

Cratinus, less grateful for the honour done to his past achievements, than indignant at the disparagement thrown on his present decline, produced, at the age of ninety-seven, his comedy of the *Flask*, and carried off the first prize against the *Clouds* of Aristophanes, which, in the judgment of Aristophanes himself, was the best of all his comedies. Aristophanes was third in this contest, Amipsias being second with his *Konnos.**

In the *Flask*, Cratinus introduced Comœdia, as his wife, seeking a divorce from him on the ground of his having neglected her, and giving himself up to his mistress, Metha, which signifies not drunkenness, but addiction to drink ; the *Beuverye* of Rabelais.† Here, as in many other Greek dramas, the taste

---

* Konnos was the preceptor of Socrates. The purpose of this comedy, like that of the *Clouds*, was probably to laugh at Socrates. In a fragment which appears to belong to it, Socrates is called " best of the few, and vainest of the many," and is praised, perhaps ironically, for his fortitude in going about with a threadbare cloak and worn-out shoes, yet, with all this manifest poverty, never condescending to flatter. *Vain* is here used, not in our ordinary sense of the adjective, but in that which we give it when we say adverbially *in vain*. Labour in vain. Coming to nothingness. This is the sense of " Vanity of vanities," in *Ecclesiastes*. Socrates is addressed as the best of the few—the few being the good ; but at the same time, as a singularly useless member of the State ; the most remarkable specimen of a man taking much trouble with no result.

† Qui feut premier, soif ou beuverye? Soif: car qui eust beu sans soif durant le temps dinnocence ? Beuverye : car *privatio præsupponit habitum.*—L. i. c. 5.

of the Athenians for judicial pleadings may have
been largely indulged, in the advocacy of their respective claims by Comœdia and Metha, each
holding that Cratinus belonged exclusively to her.

The fragments of this comedy are few and brief;
but they throw some light on its scope and
progress.

The first two in order are from a speech of
Comœdia.

I.

Now I would turn attention to this question,—
Whether, being thus devoted to a rival,
To her, and for her he calumniates me?
Old age and wine have wrought this change upon him,
That he thinks nothing equal to his Metha.

II.

Once I was his dear wife, but now no more so.

The Athenians mixed water with their wine, and
to this practice that of Cratinus himself was not an
exception. Comœdia, in the next fragment, represents him as so absorbed in his favourite beverage,
that all his ideas, even of female beauty, were expressed in images drawn from it.

III.

Now if he looks upon a youthful beauty,
He asks, if one of her to three of water
Would be a pleasant mixture?

Cratinus begins his reply by something like a
forensic formula, of which several examples are
adduced from Greek orators.

IV.

You see the preparation and the purpose.

That is, you see how my adversary has got up the case against me. He then proceeds to repudiate the mixture of one to three, which had been assumed to be his taste.

V.

I like not one to three, but half and half.

And then ¡vindicates his taste for wine by the sentence :—

VI.

A water-drinker brings forth nothing wise.

This line has been preserved by the author of an epigram in Athenæus.*

" ' Nought wise a water-drinker's brain can spin ; '
So sang our old Cratinus in his jollity,
Redolent daily, not of one good skin,
But a whole barrel of the choicest quality.

" ' Wine is the poet's Pegasus,' he said.
Through all his house were Bacchic garlands spread,
And ivy wreathed his brow, like Bacchus's own head."

As an illustration of his proposition, the wine that is in him overflows in a splendid dithyrambic, which draws from one of the interlocutors the following expressions of admiration :—

VII.

Oh, King Apollo ! what a stream of words !
The springs resound : from his twelve-fountained throat
Ilissus rolls in flood. What can I say?

* P. 39, c.

1

Unless some stop his mouth, the gushing torrent
Will bear down all before it.

After this, Comœdia appears to have been asked
how, if the judgment were given in her favour, she
would keep her husband sober?

VIII.

—How, how can any one
Keep him from drink? from too much drink?

COMŒDIA.

I know.
I will come down like lightning on his wine-tubs :
Burn up his casks to ashes : smash all vessels
That minister to drink : he shall not have
So much unbroken as a vinegar-cruet.

Meincke thinks that Cratinus becomes penitent,
returns to his first wife, and dismisses Metha ;
which he infers from the next fragment :—

IX.

I feel and own my wickedness and folly.

But we cannot see more in this, than repentance
for having altogether discarded Comœdia, and
taken exclusively to Metha. No. Cratinus remained what he was to the last : or Aristophanes
could never have said that he died of a broken
heart on seeing the running to waste of a barrel of
wine which had been fractured in a Lacedæmonian
incursion.

The other fragments are short, and throw little
light on the subject, and we cannot state from
evidence the termination of the fable. Nevertheless, we think the premises, as we have them, point

to only one conclusion. Comœdia and Metha each severally pleaded her exclusive right to Cratinus ; Cratinus demonstrated that his devotion to Comœdia would be unavailing without the inspiration of Metha ; and they finished, like the heroines of a German tragedy, by agreeing to live in harmony with the hero and each other.

There are some traces of a festival, in which Cratinus eats and drinks abundantly, and which probably, with its festal songs, wound up the drama.

We may presume the comedy to have contained some choice dithyrambics, not only in the torrent of verse poured forth by Cratinus himself, and so singularly panegyrized in a passage previously cited, but in the choral odes ; and that in these Bacchus was celebrated conjointly with the Athenians, as in the few fragments of the dithyrambics of Pindar which have been spared to us.

The Greek Bacchic Chorus grew out of the songs of the vintage ; recitations between the choral songs grew into dialogues, and progressively into the drama. Cratinus is justly regarded as the father of the Old Comedy. It is claimed for him, as for Æschylus in Tragedy, that he was the first who established order in the disposition of the scenes, limiting the number of the speakers to three : which Horace lays down as a rule of the drama : *Nec quarta loqui persona laboret ;* and that from jokes, which had aimed only at exciting laughter, he took to lashing public and private vice

in all its forms, and administered his flagellations
with more justice than mercy. The Old Comedy
thus became a mighty instrument of moral and
political censure, and the satiric rod was wielded
most effectively by Cratinus, Eupolis, and Aristophanes, whom both Horace and Persius cite as
their three great precursors in the poetical denuncia-
tion of rascals. The Old Comedians had, in fact,
an unlimited lawful authority to say whatever they
pleased of anybody : they spared neither gods nor
men ; and they exercised, during about sixty-four
years, a very salutary control over profligates and
demagogues, till the licence degenerated into
abuse ; or, in other words, became obnoxious to
parties in the State who had sufficient power to
coerce it.

Our present purpose, however, is not with the
moral and political censorship exercised by the Old
Comedy, but with the doctrine of which the
" Flask " furnishes the text—the necessary depend-
ence of good poetry on good liquor.

Homer's Demodocus has a cup of wine by him,*
to drink as his mind may direct. Hercules, the
finest gentleman of antiquity, according to Lord
Monboddo,†—and though not himself a poet, one
of the greatest subjects of poetry—is distinctly
characterised by his love of strong potations.

Wordsworth, though himself a water-drinker,

* Odyss. viii. 70.
† " Horace, who was, after Hercules, the finest gentleman
of antiquity."

could sympathise with Fancy and Feeling in their Bacchic expression, and could not resist the pleasure of transcribing a portion of an ode,* in which Cotton represents himself garrisoning his little castle with jolly fellows, and fortifying it with old sack against the artillery of winter.

Wordsworth's own genius is in no respect Bacchic : it is neither epic, nor dramatic, nor dithyrambic. He has deep thought and deep feeling, graceful imaginings, great pathos, and little passion. Withal, his Muse is as decorous as Pamela, much of a Vestal, and nothing of a Bacchant. Therefore, though we have cited him as a witness, we shall not treat him as either plaintiff or defendant in the cause.

The inspiration of lyrical poetry by wine might be amply illustrated by the theory and practice of its greatest masters, from Alcæus downwards. The Old Comedy was in its origin essentially lyrical, and never lost sight of its Bacchic birth ; and though the personal history of many of its brightest ornaments is obscure, yet, as far as positive evi-

---

* In the preface to the edition of his poems published in 1815. The passage referred to above immediately precedes the verses quoted by Wordsworth :

> Fly, fly : the foe advances fast
> Into our fortress let us haste,
> Where all the roarers of the north
> Can neither storm nor starve us forth.
> There underground a magazine
> Of sovereign juice is cellared in :
> Liquor that will the siege maintain,
> Should Phœbus ne'er return again.

dence goes, there is not a single water-drinker among them.

We have shown the Father of Comedy as a devotee of Bacchus. According to Athenæus, the Father of Tragedy was no less so, and never wrote when he was sober : which led Sophocles to say to him, " Oh, Æschylus! if what you do you do well, you do it, not knowing what you do." * And Æschylus occasionally justified his practice by making his heroes do the same. For example, in the Cabiri, he brought Jason and his companions gloriously drunk on the stage ; and in the very small remnants we have of this drama, we find them threatening to drink up all the wine in the place so thoroughly, that they will not leave even a drop of vinegar.

Sophocles, though he blamed Æschylus for over-indulgence in wine, was nevertheless far from anti-Bacchic in his habits. We find him at Chios very facetious in his cups. †

Euripides was not given to merriment ; he has been called ἀγέλαστος, the unlaughing, as his pre-ceptor, Anaxagoras, had been before him, and as subsequently was Crassus, the grandfather of the Triumvir ; who is said never to have laughed but once, which was at a joke of his own cracking, on the congeniality of the lips and the lettuce, when he saw an ass eating thistles. ‡ Whereon Cicero observes, that this single exception does

---

* Athenæus, p. 428, f.   † Id., p. 603, f.
‡ *Similem habent labra lactucam.*

not take away his title to the appellation. Euripides
is accused by Alexander Ætolus—who calls him
μισογέλως, laughter-hating—of not enlivening wine
with jests ; * but this shows that he did drink
wine, though he was not facetious in his cups like
Sophocles. And we may observe, incidentally,
that those who hold tragedy to have progressively
degenerated from its original grandeur in Æschylus,
cannot deny the simultaneous diminution of the
Bacchic inspiration. At the same time, we nowhere
find more splendid panegyrics on good liquor, and
its influence on the enjoyment of life, than in the
dramas of Euripides, especially the "Bacchæ"
and "Cyclops," and the speech of Hercules to the
Attendant, in the "Alcestis : "

> Ho you ! why look you thus solemn and thoughtful ?
> It ill becomes a servant to meet guests
> With gloomy looks ; their due is cordial service.
> Here you receive your master's ancient friend
> With dismal aspect and contracted brows,
> Bending your mind to some extraneous grief,
> Come here, that you may grow a wiser man.
> Know you the nature of all mortal things?
> No ! whence should you have learned it ? Listen, then :
> To all mankind death is the foreshown doom ;
> Nor is there one of all who live to-day,
> That knows if he shall see to-morrow's dawn.
> There is no art to pierce the clouds, that hide
> The end to which the steps of Fortune lead.
> Now having heard and learned thus much from me,
> Make glad your spirit : drink : the passing day
> Esteem your own, and all the rest as Fortune's.

* Aulus Gellius ; xv. 20.

Worship especially the sweetest Power
Of Heaven to mortal men : benignant Venus.
Leave useless cares, and profit by my words,
If right you deem them, as I think you must do.
Adorn your head with wreaths, and cross this threshold
To drink with me ; and well I know the bowl,
Sparkling with joyous impulses, will drive you
Out of this dark contraction of your mind.
Men should learn wisdom from mortality ;
And 'tis my judgment that to all who pass
Their days with solemn looks and pursed-up brows,
Life is not truly life, but mere calamity.

Of the habits of Eupolis we have no direct evidence ; but as he was *il terzo fra cotanto senno—*
second in time—of the three great names of the
Old Comedy—

> *Eubolis, atque Cratinus, Aristophanesque poëtæ,**

we may presume that if he had formed anything
like a contrast to the other two, it would have
been recorded as a phenomenon.

Aristophanes himself, notwithstanding his jokes
on the vinosity of Cratinus, is said in Athenæus †
to have been well primed with wine when he sat
down to write.‡ And as Aristophanes has taken,

* Persius's enumeration is more strictly chronological :

> *audaci quicumque afflate Cratino*
> *Iratum Eupolidem prægrandi cum sene palles.*

† P. 429, a.

‡ Rabelais took after his masters of the Old Comedy : "A
la composition de ce livre seigneurial, je ne perdy ne em·
ployai oncques plus ny aultre temps que celluy qui estoit
establi a prendre ma refection corporelle, scavoir est, beuvant
et mangeant. Aussi est-ce la juste heure descripre ces haultes
matières et sciences profundes."—Prol. l. i.

in fame, the lead of his predecessors, it may be said that the progress of comic genius kept pace with that of the Bacchic inspiration.

So much for the great masters of the Athenian theatre. The Middle Comedy was less poetical than the Old, and the New than the Middle; and with these we descend progressively into a more and more temperate region.

In the Middle Comedy, the Chorus appears to have first lost its lyrical character, and finally to have disappeared altogether. In the New Comedy, the Chorus has no place. The Middle Comedy, being interdicted from personal and political satire, turned back on the mythical ages, and brought forward gods and heroes; not perhaps without some covert glances at the present under the semblance of the past. This was precisely the plan on which Juvenal proposed to act. As Tigellinus could not be touched with impunity, he would try what could be made of Æneas and Turnus, Achilles, Hylas, and the Nymphs, and the more recent and real men whose ashes reposed along the Appian and Flaminian Ways.

Even this course, however, was not altogether safe. For though the story that Anaxandrides was starved to death, by the sentence of an Athenian tribunal, for a libel on the city, rests on no solid foundation, it is certain that the shadowing out of men in power, under names of departed heroes, could not but have been attended with peril if the audience perceived the application. Thus the

Middle Comedy gradually subsided into pictures
of manners and characters of everyday life, to
which the New Comedy was exclusively devoted.
But both abound with praises of conviviality.
The remains of the Middle Comedy are redolent
of festivity, and the New Comedy supplied, according to Plutarch, "the greatest number of pleasant
things to be heard as accompaniments to suppers,
with which it was so mixed up, that it seemed as
if they could be more easily carried through without wine than without Menander; pleasant things,
in sweet and familiar diction, worthy to be heard
by the sober, with nothing to annoy, and much to
delight the jovial.* We do not construe this too
literally, as implying that wine had ceased to be
indispensable at suppers, for it is not easy to
conceive the jovial as receiving delight from anything else in its absence; but we take it as a
strong expression of the great pleasure which was
added to banquets, by recitations of pleasant passages from the favourite poet of the New Comedy.

At the same time it must be admitted, that in
these second and third forms of comedy, everything is more temperate and subdued than in their
vigorous and fiery precursor. We find in them
even praises of water-drinking. Eubulus (Middle
Comedy) says—"Pure water-drinkers are inven-
tive; wine clouds the mind;" a passage which
is certainly ἀπροσδιόνυσον. But the interlocutor in
Athenæus immediately subjoins an opposite quota-

* *Quæst. Symp.* viii. 3, p. 712, b.

tion from Amphis (also Middle Comedy), to the effect, that there is a power of discourse in wine, and that the genius of water-drinkers is stupefied by their thin potations.

There are, however, more praises of temperance in wine than of pure water-drinking. Thus, there are many recommendations to mix it with water,*

* Lord Monboddo, whose tastes were all Greek, warmly advocates this mixed liquor : " As by Isis a plant was discovered which furnished bread to man, so by Osiris, her husband and brother, an art was invented of making a drink for man. This art is what is called *fermentation*, which he applied to the juice of the grape ; and so first made wine, which,' although it has been very much abused (as almost every production of nature and art has been by man), and therefore is very properly styled by Milton, *The sweet poison of misused wine*, may be applied to the most useful purposes ; for it is the best cordial of old age, and at all times of life it enlivens the spirits, and therefore Bacchus is called by Virgil *Lætitiæ dator*, and it cherishes the stomach. But it is a great abuse of this liquor in modern times, to drink it pure, without mixture of water, which I am sorry to observe so much practised in Britain, where port, a wine full as strong as the best Greek wine, the Chian (as I am informed by a gentleman who has been in Greece and often drank of that wine), is drunk without any mixture of water, which makes it very inflammatory and intoxicating ; whereas wine, properly mixed with water, is a much better drink than pure water, for it corrects the coldness and crudity of the water, and, I am persuaded, invigorates the stomach, and makes it more easily digest that unnatural diet, as I call it, *flesh*. It is therefore true what Solomon has said, *That wine without water is not good, nor water without wine ; but both together make an excellent drink.* The ancient Greeks and Romans, as they did not drink wine without water, so neither did they

and always more than half and half. Eubulus
introduces Bacchus himself, saying even of this
mixed liquor :

> Three cups, no more, I mix for prudent guests :
> The first for health : the next for love and pleasure :
> The third for sleep, which being drained, the wise
> Will hasten home. The fourth is not for us,
> But insolence : the fifth belongs to clamour :
> The sixth to riotous merriment : the seventh
> To jeers : the eighth to rows, and summoners
> In law : the ninth to wrath : the tenth to madness,
> Fighting, with bowls for missiles. Thus, much wine,
> Poured into one small vessel, trips up equally
> The minds and heels of the drinkers.

Philemon, second only to Menander among the
authors of the New Comedy, was himself a model
of temperance (it does not appear that he was a
water-drinker), and lived more than a century; but

drink water without wine, if they could get wine ; and the
Roman soldier, who could not afford wine, rather than drink
pure water, mixed vinegar with it, and made of it a liquor
called *Posca*. Virgil, therefore, has very properly described
the use of wine, when, speaking of Bacchus, he has said :

> Poculaque inventis Acheloïa miscuit uvis.

The ancient Greeks, therefore, never drank it pure, even in
the heroic ages, when they were so much bigger and stronger
than in aftertimes. The Romans also mixed it with water,
and Horace calls loudly for it :

> ———— Quis puer ocyus
> Restinguet ardentis Falerni
> Pocula prætereunte lymphâ ? "
> *Ancient Metaphysics*, vol iv. p. 141.

Cratinus, with all his jollity, had nearly completed one. The Old Comedy, though not all poetry, abounded with poetry of the highest order. The New Comedy never soared into the sky, to build a Cuckoo-city-in-the-Clouds ; nor ferried over the Styx, beating time with its oars to the accompaniment of a chorus of frogs. It stood quietly on earth, and held the mirror up to human life. The Muses of the Old Comedy were never found without Bacchus. For Cratinus, their Hippocrene ran wine. But, before Philemon came on the stage, Bacchus, Silenus, and the Satyrs had left it. They left it, in fact, with the lyrical Chorus, and returned to it no more as the presiding powers of the theatre. But they shed their influence on Ennius, the Father of Latin poetry, both epic and dramatic. We have seen, in the motto to this article, how well he kept up the Dionysiac succession. The motto begins with Cratinus, and ends with Ennius. We shall for the present go no farther than our text, and we might conclude with applying to this point what Persius applied to another, in a very happy expression, as if the glorious old poet had been all heart :

Cor jubet hoc Enni.
So bids the heart of Ennius.

But as we have given one or two views of the other side of the question, we will terminate with the most striking—from a congenial source, the Old Sicilian Comedy—the often-quoted sentiment of Epicharmus. This is, in the original, a single line ;

but it is a trochaic tetrameter, and its full meaning
cannot be expressed, like that of Cratinus's senarius,
in one.   We therefore give it in two :

> Be sober, and not lightly credulous :
> These are the nerves and sinews of the mind.

THE LAST DAY OF WINDSOR FOREST.

[The original MS. of the following paper is extant among the MS. remains of the author, the late Thomas Love Peacock, and is the only one of them absolutely complete and ready for publication. It was in all probability intended for *Fraser's Magazine*, but never appeared there, nor, so far as can be discovered, elsewhere. The probable date of composition is about 1862.

Apart from the literary merit of the paper, and its interest as a record of forgotten circumstances, it is a fitting conclusion to the literary life of the veteran author, ending it where it may be said to have begun. Peacock's first and only school had been at Englefield Green, on the verge of Windsor Forest, and there he imbibed that love for river and sylvan scenery in general, and for that of the Thames and Windsor in particular, which colours nearly all his writings.—*National Magazine*, Aug. 1887.—R. G.]

MANY of my younger, and some of my maturer years, were passed on the borders of Windsor Forest. I was early given to long walks and rural explorations, and there was scarcely a spot of the Park or the Forest with which I was not intimately acquainted. There were two very different scenes to which I was especially attached: Virginia Water, and a dell near Winkfield Plain.

The bank of Virginia Water, which the public enter from the Wheatsheaf Inn, is bordered, between the cascade to the left and the iron gates to the right, by groves of trees, which, with the exception of a few old ones near the water, have grown up within my memory. They were planted by George the Third, and the entire space was called the King's Plantation. Perhaps they were more beautiful in an earlier stage than they are now; or I may so think and feel, through the general preference of the past to the present, which seems inseparable from old age. In my first acquaintance with the place, and for some years subsequently, sitting in the large upper room of the Inn, I could look on the cascade and the expanse of the lake, which have long been masked by trees.

Virginia Water was always open to the public, through the Wheatsheaf Inn, except during the regency and reign of George the Fourth, who not only shut up the grounds, but enclosed them, where they were open to a road, with higher fences than even the outside passengers of stage-coaches could look over, that he might be invisible in his punt, while fishing on the lake. William the Fourth lowered the fences, and re-opened the old access.

While George the Third was King, Virginia Water was a very solitary place. I have been there day after day, without seeing another visitor. Now it has many visitors. It is a source of great enjoyment to many, though no longer suitable to *Les Reveries d'un Promeneur Solitaire.*

A still more solitary spot, which had especial charms for me, was the deep forest dell already mentioned, on the borders of Winkfield Plain. This dell, I think, had the name of the Bourne ; but I always called it the Dingle. In the bottom was a watercourse, which was a stream only in times of continuous rain. Old trees clothed it on both sides to the summit, and it was a favourite resort of deer. I was a witness of their banishment from their forest haunts. The dell itself remained some time unchanged ; but I have not seen it since 1815, when I frequently visited it in company with Shelley, during his residence at Bishopgate, on the eastern side of the Park. I do not know what changes it may have since undergone. Not much, perhaps, being now a portion of the Park. But many portions of the Park and its vicinity, as well as of the immediate neighbourhood of Windsor, which were then open to the public, have ceased to be so, and such may be the case with this. I have never ventured to ascertain the point. In all the portions of the old forest, which were distributed in private allotments, I know what to expect.

I shrink from the ghosts of my old associations in scenery, and never, if I can help it, revisit an enclosed locality with which I have been familiar in its openness.

Wordsworth would not visit Yarrow, because he
feared to disappoint his imagination :

> Be Yarrow stream unseen, unknown !
> It must, or we shall rue it :
> We have a vision of our own,
> Ah ! why should we undo it ?
> The treasured dreams of times long past,
> We'll keep them, winsome Marrow !
> For when we're there, although 'tis fair,
> 'Twill be another Yarrow.*

Yet when he afterwards visited it, though it was
not what he had dreamed, he still found it beautiful,
and rejoiced in having seen it :

> The vapours linger round the heights,
> They melt, and soon must vanish ;
> One hour is theirs, nor more is mine
> Sad thought which I would banish,
> But that I know, where'er I go,
> Thy genuine image, Yarrow !
> Will dwell with me to heighten joy
> And cheer my mind in sorrow.†

He found compensation in the reality for the
difference of imagined scene ; but there is no such
compensation for the disappointments of memory ;
and where—in the place of scenes of youth, where
we have wandered under antique trees, through
groves and glades, through bushes and underwood,
among fern, and fox-glove, and bounding deer ;
where, perhaps, every "minutest circumstance of
place" has been not only "as a friend" in itself,
but has recalled some association of early friend-

* *Yarrow Unvisited.*   † *Yarrow Visited,*

ship, or youthful love—we can only pass between high fences and dusty roads ; I think it best to avoid the sight of the reality, and to make the best of cherishing at a distance

> The memory of what has been,
> And never more will be.—*Wordsworth.*

I do not express, or imply, any opinion on the general utility of enclosures. For the most part, they illustrate the Scriptural maxim : " To him that hath much, much shall be given ; and from him that hath little, shall be taken away even the little he hath." They are like most events in this world, " Good to some, bad to others, and indifferent to the majority." They are good to the land-owner, who gets an addition to his land ; they are bad to the poor parishioner, who loses his rights of common ; they are bad to the lover of rural walks, for whom footpaths are annihilated ; they are bad to those for whom the scenes of their youth are blotted from the face of the world. These last are of no account in ledger balances, which profess to demonstrate that the loss of the poor is more than counterbalanced by the gain of the rich ; that the aggregate gain is the gain of the community ; and that all matters of taste and feeling are fitly represented by a cypher. So be it.

George the Fourth's exclusions and high fences had not, however, effectually secured to him the secrecy he desired. On an eminence outside of the royal grounds, stood, and still stands, in the midst of a pine-grove, a tower, which, from its form, was commonly called the Clock-Case. This tower, and the land round it, had been sold for a small sum, as a lot in a sale of Crown Lands. The tower was in two or three stories, and was inhabited by a poor family, who had a telescope, supplied, most probably, by the new proprietor, on the platform of the roof, which rose high above the trees, and commanded an extensive view of the lake. This tower and its grounds became a place of great resort for picnic parties, and visitors of all kinds, who kept up a perpetual succession at the telescope, while the Royal Angler and his fair companion were fishing. This became an intolerable nuisance to the would-be recluse. He set on foot a negotiation for re-purchasing the Clock-Case. The sum demanded was many times the multiple of the purchase money. The demand was for some time resisted, but the proprietor was inflexible. The sum required was paid, the property reverted to the Crown, and the public were shut out from the Clock-Case and its territory. When William the Fourth succeeded, this story was told to him, and he said : " A good place for a view, is it ? I will put an old couple into it, and give them a telescope ; " which was done without loss of time. I saw and conversed with this old couple, and looked through their telescope.

About the same time, William the Fourth was sitting one Sunday evening in a window of Windsor Castle, when the terrace was thronged with people.

A heavy rain came on, and the people ran in all directions. He said to someone near him, "This is the strangest thing I ever saw : so many English people, without an umbrella among them." He was told that by order of his late Majesty, umbrellas were prohibited on the terrace. "Then," he said, "let the prohibition be immediately withdrawn."

In the early days of his reign he was fond of walking about, not only in Windsor, but in London. It pleased him to be among the people. In one of his walks he noticed in Windsor Little Park, a board with an inscription by which all persons were " ordered " to keep the footpath. He desired that "requested " might be substituted. He was told that "requested " would not be attended to. He said : " If they will not attend to 'requested,' that is their affair ; I will not have 'ordered.' "

A most good-natured, kind-hearted gentleman was William the Fourth ; but to record the many instances of good feeling in his sayings and doings, which came within my knowledge, would be foreign to the purpose of the present paper.

The Act for the enclosure of Windsor Forest contained the following clause :—

WINDSOR FOREST, 53rd Geo. III. cap. 158.

LXIV.—And be it further enacted, that from and after the first day of July one thousand eight hundred and fourteen, all and singular the Lands, Tenements and Hereditaments within the said respective Parishes and Liberties (save and except such Parts thereof respectively as are now

or shall or may become vested in His Majesty, or any Person
or Persons in Trust for Him by virtue hereof) shall be, and
the same is and are hereby, disafforested to all Intents and
Purposes whatsoever ; and that from thenceforth no Person
or Persons shall be questioned or liable to any Pain, Penalty
or Punishment for hunting, coursing, killing, destroying, or
taking any Deer whatsoever within the same, save and
except within such Part or Parts thereof (if any) as shall be
enclosed with Pales and kept for a Park or Parks by the
Owners, Lessees, or Tenants thereof.

There can be little doubt that the exception in
favour of the Crown was intended to apply to all
the provisions of the clause ; but it was held by
Counsel learned in the law that it applied to the
first half only, and that after the specified day it
was lawful to kill deer in any portion of the old
forest not enclosed with pales, whether such portion
had or had not been vested in the Crown. The
Crown allotment had been left as it was.

Armed with this opinion, a farmer of Water
Oakley, whose real I have forgotten in his assumed
name, calling himself Robin Hood, and taking
with him two of his men, whom he called Scarlet
and Little John, sallied forth daily into the forest
to kill the King's deer, and returned home every
evening loaded with spoil.

Lord Harcourt, who was then Deputy Ranger
of the Forest, and discharged all the duties of
superintendence (for the Ranger, who was a Royal
Highness, of course, did nothing), went forth also,
as the representative of Majesty, to put down these
audacious trespassers.   In my forest rambles I was

a witness to some of their altercations:—Lord
Harcourt threatening to ruin Robin Hood by process in the Court of Exchequer; Robin Hood
setting him at defiance, flourishing the Act of
Parliament, and saying, "My Lord, if you don't
know how to make Acts of Parliament, I'll teach
you."

One day I was walking towards the Dingle, when
I met a man with a gun, who asked me if I had
seen Robin Hood? I said I had just seen him at
a little distance in discussion with Lord Harcourt,
who was on horse-back, Robin Hood being on
foot. He asked me to point out the direction,
which I did; and in return, I asked him who he
might be. He told me he was Scarlet. He was
a pleasant-looking man, and seemed as merry as
his original: like one in high enjoyment of
sport.

This went on some time. The law was not
brought to bear on Robin Hood, and it was finally
determined to settle the matter by driving the deer
out of the forest into the park. Two regiments of
cavalry were employed for this purpose, which was
kept as secret as possible, for a concourse of people
would have been a serious impediment to the
operation.

I received intelligence of it from a friend at
court, who pointed out to me a good position from
which to view the close of the proceedings.

My position was on a rising ground, covered
with trees, and overlooking an extensive glade.

The park was on my left hand, the main part of
the forest on the right and before me. A wide
extent of the park paling had been removed, and
rope fencing had been carried to a great length, at
oblique angles from the opening. It was a clear,
calm sunny day, and for a time there was profound
silence. This was first broken by the faint sound
of bugles, answering each other's signals from
remote points in the distance; drawing nearer by
degrees, and growing progressively loud. Then
came two or three straggling deer, bounding from
the trees, and flying through the opening of the park
pales. Then came greater numbers, and ultimately
congregated herds; the beatings of their multitudinous feet mingled with the tramplings of the yet
unseen horses, and the full sounds of the bugles.
Last appeared the cavalry, issuing from the woods,
and ranging themselves in a semi-circle, from horn
to horn of the rope fencing. The open space was
filled with deer, terrified by the chase, confused by
their own numbers, and rushing in all directions,
the greater part through the park opening; many
trying to leap the rope fencing, in which a few
were hurt; and one or two succeeded, escaping to
their old haunts, most probably to furnish Robin
Hood with his last venison feast. By degrees the
mass grew thinner; at last all had disappeared,
the rope fencing shut up the park for the night,
the cavalry rode off towards Windsor, and all again
was silent.

This was, without any exception, the most beautiful sight I ever witnessed; but I saw it with deep regret, for, with the expulsion of the deer, the life of the old scenes was gone, and I have always looked back on that day as the last day of Windsor Forest.

INDEX TO FIRST LINES OF SONGS.

ERRATA.

HEADLONG HALL.

P. 17, six lines from bottom, *for* "Seythrop" *read* "Scythrop."

P. 21, l. 4, *for* "words" *read* "winds."

P. 39, l. 17, *for* "*in sto*" *read* "*insto.*"

MELINCOURT.

Preface, p. 8, l. 13, *for* "Natural" *read* "National."

P. 7, *for* "incontestible" read "incontestable."

MAID MARIAN.

Preface, p. 9, l. 20, *for* "jocund" *read* "second."

P. 19, *for* "Mistress" read "Huntress."

GRYLL GRANGE.

Preface, l. 1, *for* "ist" *read* "ist's."

P. 1, l. 11, *dele comma after* "too."

TURNBULL AND SPEARS, PRINTERS, EDINBURGH.